E.

Written by Carole Kohn

This novel is a work of fiction. Names, characters, businesses, places, events and incidents are either the products of the author's imagination or used in a fictitious manner. Any resemblance to actual persons, living or dead, or actual events is purely coincidental.

Karen Sullivan, Editor
Amanda Grieme, Design

CHAPTER ONE

"Wanted Vocalist to Perform In E. Tribute, Must Have Baritone to Tenor Range," the ad was placed in the *Memphis Gazette*. Within hours, no less than 14 appointments were made. The usual audition room was made ready for the eager performers. One mic, two speakers, one tape recorder and a camcorder were in place. The first man to audition was Jose Maraquez. He was a laborer from San Jose, California who performed E. impersonations and music by the group Santana for small gatherings and supportive relatives in the Chicano community where he lived. He was marked off as unacceptable before he even opened his mouth. Number two, a nineteen year old who wiggled his hips and strained to hit the high notes on "American Trilogy" also was rejected. Number three was a woman in a red jump suit, who sang while playing her own accompaniment on a guitar. So went the day. Fourteen showed. Two were strongly considered.

Marlene Hardison, who judged the auditions, ran the corporate offices. At forty-two years old, thanks to the help of extensive cosmetic surgery, hundreds of dollars of make-up and a religious exercise program, she could pass for thirty-five. Now, as she thanked each auditioner for coming by, picked up her brief case and walked into the ladies room, she felt her age. Applying some powder to her face, she thought about how young she had been the first time she had met E.

She was in sales at Winchester Motors, the most prestigious Cadillac dealership in Memphis. E. and his friends arrived at the dealership on a weekday, a few minutes before closing. Almost knocking down another salesman, she rushed to wait on him. By the time the sale was complete, E. had purchased two new Eldorados. He paid cash for both of these Cadillacs. Then, much to her pleasure, he had posed for a picture. Putting his arm around her waist and looking into her eyes, he asked her to think about coming to work for him at The Mansion. Marlene remained long enough at the dealership to mount his photo on their sales wall and collect her commission. Then she took the job that had been offered to her. As far as she knew, the picture of the two of them still hung on the dealership's wall.

    E. made it a point to show her around The Mansion and to treat her with his usual charm. Puzzled by her coolness, he ordered one of his boys to check into her personal life. Within a week he had his answer. On his desk was a black and white photo of Marlene. She was in the heavy embrace of another woman. E. never got over this. Marlene knew he had discovered her secret. But, neither brought up the touchy subject. To this day she remained strictly office staff.

    Back in her office, Marlene called the two lucky impersonators, informing them that they should return the next morning for a second audition. This time, on the other side of a one-way glass, her boss would do the final judging.

E. looked better today. He had slept for two hours after breakfast. Dressed in his blue silk shirt, black pants and bike boots, he settled into the leather recliner. Jerry asked him if he wanted some coffee. As E. answered him, he noticed that he looked rested and didn't stutter this morning. Even his dark circles and heavy eyelids didn't seem so pronounced in the dim light of the observation room. For a moment, Jerry wished they didn't have to go through with this.

Eddie Arroyo posed behind the mike, his feet spread wide, his arms open. As the music played, he gave it all he had. Finishing an impressive rendition of the required "American Trilogy" he looked expectantly at Marlene. Smiling, she told him to sit down at the card table in the far corner of the room. His knee bounced with anxiety, as the other man walked up to the mike. E. watched Eddie through the glass.

"Man, do I look that bad?" He laughed as he stared at the visibly nervous Eddie.

Jerry pretended not to hear. The second auditioner was belting out another stunning version of the "American Trilogy" and Jerry's head was throbbing. As the second man finished, E. turned to Jerry.

"Now that's better. At least he looks like me."

The second performer, Cliff Settle, did look like him. He looked like E. at one hundred and seventy pounds. Cliff's resume stated that he was a body builder and his physique confirmed that. Unfortunately, he didn't look like the man who was sitting in the observation room with Jerry.

"E., be realistic, he's not going to work," Jerry said, getting up from his stool by the window and walking out into the audition room.

Marlene looked expectantly in his direction. Shaking each performer's hand, he dismissed the two impersonators. His decision had been made and Marlene could take it from here.

Eddie Arroyo left the mansion feeling good about his audition.

"The other guy has a good build, but he sure doesn't have my voice. No, he isn't right. I'm the man," he said, convincing himself.

That feeling of power stayed with Eddie as he opened the door of his one bedroom apartment at the Winchester Arms. The phone was ringing. Hurrying across the kitchen, he picked up the phone on the third ring. The smile slid from his face, as he heard the shrill voice of his boss. He had worked for K-Mart Industries for the last two years and knew better than to answer the phone on his day off. Someone had called in sick and he had to go into the bathroom. Washing the dark eyebrow pencil from his brows and changing into his white shirt and red vest he wished it had been Marlene on the phone.

On his break he told his best friend, Steve, about his audition. Steve leaned close to Eddy and whispered, "Hey man, I'd think twice before leaving here. Jobs are hard to find, especially with benefits."

By ten-thirty Eddie had lost all his confidence. As he started his 1965 Chevy and pulled out of the dark K-Mart parking lot, he didn't notice the two men, in the new 1975 Cadillac, that were following him. They followed him down Winchester, past the strip clubs off Brookes Road and chuckled out loud when he made a left turn and headed past the mansion.

"This guy's got it bad. He can't go home without checking to see if E.'s still awake. "Asshole. Oh well, that just makes our job easier."

Eddie thought about stopping at his favorite bar, "The Robin's Nest" for a beer. It was after eleven. Even with all the windows down in his car, it was hot and sticky. As he turned into the gravel driveway and parked below the flashing neon beer sign, he noticed the shiny blue caddy turning around in the driveway of the bar.

"Man, someday I'm goin' to have a big-assed caddy with air," he swore.

He didn't notice the two men in the front seat and he didn't see the flash from their camera, as he entered the bar.

It was after ten the next morning when Eddie heard the phone ringing in his kitchen. He lay nude on top of the damp sheets wondering if he should answer it. He wasn't due into work until two and the way his head felt, he wasn't even sure he was going. The bar had been hopping last night. They were having a Karaoke Contest. He hadn't performed. But, he had drunk enough beer that he found the other performers took care of both of them. Marlene loved her job and having the financial control over her relationship gave her a secure feeling. But this last assignment was the craziest thing she had ever become involved in. "Oh well," she thought. "Whatever E. wants, E. gets!"

Regaining her composure she told Eddie that he didn't need to bring his tracks with him. He was to be at the corporate offices at six and to bring his social security card and his driver's license.

"Miss Hardison," Eddie asked pensively, "does this mean I got the job?"

"I'm not at liberty to divulge that information," she said, loving every minute of this cat and mouse game. "However, I think if I was voting, I would vote for you."

He hiked up his towel up on his hips and assured her he would be there by six.

Standing nude in front of the full-length mirror in the bathroom, Eddie surveyed his thirty-seven year old body. He weighed two hundred and fifty pounds and was almost six feet tall. His arms were well muscled and he did have a striking resemblance to E. Doing a couple of E.'s famous poses, using the bath towel for his cape, he broke into a loud rendition of "Hound Dog," ending his song with the now famous, "thank-you, thank-you very much" drawl.

It was well past noon when Eddie remembered to call his job. Pretending to be sick, he told Sheila, the manager that he wouldn't be able to come to work. She listened to his feeble excuse of a bad headache and a sick stomach and with her usual lack of sincerity, told him she hoped he got well real soon. He could see her already calling another unlucky employee on his day off, forcing them to cover his shift. He didn't care. He was going to the mansion.

CHAPTER TWO

Marlene sorted through the paperwork that the detective had left on her desk. Eddie Arroyo had no warrants against him. He had been with K-Mart Industries for the last two years. He was divorced. His ex-wife lived in Michigan. She had remarried three years ago. His two children lived with their mom and step-dad and according to the courts, Eddie had not paid child support for the last three years. She was sure that his wife had no idea that he was in Memphis.

"Well, well, well, another dead-beat dad. Perfect," she said, as she closed the folder and lit a cigarette.

"I thought you gave those up?" asked the fat detective who returned to Marlene's office, drinking a chocolate milk-shake.

"No, and I don't suppose I ever will," she sighed. "Working here isn't exactly relaxing."

"When's he do in? I was told to wait here. But, if it's going to be much later, I'm going to run over to Whimpy's and get a burger. Want anything?"

Marlene shook her head. A burger would defeat her latest diet. It was past five and the attorneys should be arriving soon. She placed a call to the mansion and Jerry answered.

"Hi, it's Marlene. So far all the info on Arroyo matches. He's due here by six. We will meet in the audition room. Is E. going to need anything special... food, drink, paper? O.K., I understand."

As she hung up the phone, she was startled to see Eddie Arroyo standing in the doorway. He was forty-five minutes early. Dressed in a black shirt and black Angel Flight bellbottom pants, he looked enough like E. to make her jump. As he walked clear to the desk, he could see the start of sideburns on his handsome face.

"Hi Eddie, I didn't hear you come in," she said, rising from her desk and backing him out of her office.

"Ya, I guess I'm a little early."

"Would you like a coke of coffee," Marlene offered, wondering where the girl at the front desk had disappeared.

"No ma'am, I'm fine. Can ya tell me more about these people that want to meet with me?"

"Eddie, sit down here in the outer office and I will be with you in a few minutes. Then we can sort this whole thing out. O.K.?"

Eddie sat down on a soft pink chair and listened to the music that filtered through the room. He was nervous and wished he had brought his back-up tapes. Softly, he began to sing with the music. Relaxing a little, he closed his eyes and sang louder.

"Sounds just like him," said the young girl from the front desk, snapping her gum loudly.

"Huh, oh I didn't know anyone was in the room. Thanks, do ya really think so?"

"You must be the new impersonator. Marlene said you'd be here at six. Guess ya couldn't wait. I'm Tammy. Congratulations on getting the job."

Eddie looked at the girl, his mouth slightly open. She said he had the job . . . God, he had the job! He stood up and walked over to her desk. Just as he started to ask her more about his new job, Marlene opened her office door.

"Mr. Arroyo, please come into my office," she said.

Marlene sat at her desk. Next to her sat two men in business suits. In the corner of the room was another man about sixty-five years old. They all stood up when he entered the room. Marlene did the introductions. The first two men were attorneys. The older man was Dr. Someti.

"Gentlemen, please follow me. We will go into the audition room. There is a large meeting table there and I think we will be much more comfortable," said Marlene, again backing Eddie out of her office.

Seated around the table, the attorneys opened their briefcases and placed several stacks of paperwork on the table. Dr. Someti eyed Eddie as if he was a prize bull. Marlene sat down next to Eddie and pressed her leg gently against his leg. Eddie's head throbbed. This was nothing like his interview at K-Mart. This was real show business.

"Congratulations, Eddie," said Marlene, as she picked up the first stack of paperwork.

"Thanks, you mean I got the job?"

"Yes, we are sure you will work out just fine. Now, I'm going to hush up and let these gentlemen lead you through this mound of paperwork, then Dr. Someti would like to run some medical tests on you."

"Hey, what kinda tests?" Eddie asked, looking suspiciously at the doctor.

"Oh, the usual. Drug, physical exam, nothing to worry about," she assured him.

The attorney nearest to Eddie was named Bill Owens. He was the first to talk.

"Mr. Arroyo, if everything checks out health wise, I'm sure you will be very pleased with the job. But, first you must read and sign this confidentiality contract. Basically, you will not reveal to anyone your job description, salary or association with any member of the personnel, or work-related. You will consider yourself a member of this association and that everything you do must be in the best interests of our client's reputation. Do you fully understand this?"

Eddie's mind was still on the word salary.

"Pardon me ma'am, but what does the position pay?" drawled Eddie, looking at Marlene, trying hard to sound like a southern boy.

"Eddie, we will discuss that with you after these papers are completed. I think you will be very pleased. Now, sign the paperwork for these attorneys, so we can get past this tiresome stuff and onto the fun stuff," whispered Marlene.

Eddie's heart skipped a beat. Reaching for the pen, he signed the six papers and looked at the attorneys.

"O.K., so what does the job pay?" said Eddie, no longer sounding like E.

Bill Owens looked at Eddie's anxious face. Picking up a three by five card from the table, the attorney scribbled the sum of $8,000 a month plus bonus. Slipping the paper across the table to Eddie, he smiled a sly smile. Eddie was good with people and had a huge ego. But, he physically reeled when he saw the amount.

"Man, who do I have to kill for this," said Eddie, slapping his large hand to his head.

The attorney was not listening to Eddie. He was too busy informing Mr. Arroyo about the mandatory thirty-day probationary period. Eddie couldn't take his eyes off the figure on the paper.

"What kind of bonus are you talking about," asked Eddie, afraid he was being too pushy.

"The bonus amount is dependent upon what you are required to do for the company and upon your ability to carry out your job. We will discuss this part of the agreement at a later date," answered Attorney Owens, rising from his chair and shaking Eddie's hand. "Do you have any further questions?" asked the second attorney, as he too shook Eddie's hand.

"No man, everything is great. Just great!" said Eddie, thinking about the fact that he was soon to make eight thousand dollars a month. "Eight thousand a month, how much is that a year?" thought Eddie, knowing he had never made over twenty thousand in his best years.

Marlene smiled at Eddie and motioned for him to sit down. Eddie's knees were jumping and it was hard for him to relax.

Dr. Someti looked at Eddie and smiled. At sixty-six years old, he had narrowed his practice down to a very few select clients. E. was his most famous client. He had met him ten years ago. A close friend of E.'s had called him and asked him to come to the mansion. A bad case of stomach flu had attacked everyone in the house. He brought his nurse, his antibiotics and his pillow.

"You know doc, my costume is white. Can ya stop this?" E. had asked.

One week later the doctor left the mansion. Everyone was recovering nicely and he had a new client. Dr. Someti's parents had been egg farmers. They had worked all their lives and died poor. He wanted more. Graduating from The University of Memphis, he decided to keep his practice in the South. After years of family practice, he had finally made his fortune. Having a few rich clients was far more lucrative than hundreds of poor families. Dr. Someti dedicated himself to pleasing these few clients and they rewarded him very handsomely.

"Mr. Arroyo, about your physical. I will need you to step into the other room. I have to take some blood and do a quick exam. It shouldn't take very long," said Dr. Someti.

Eddie followed the doctor into a back room, no bigger than a closet. He loved being on the grounds, but he wondered why the doctor didn't have an office downtown.

"Well Eddie, you seem to be in fine shape," said Dr. Someti, as he checked his heart and blood pressure. "Now, drop your pants and remove your shirt."

"Hey doc, what the hell? I thought I would be singing, so why the full physical?"

"Well Eddie," said the doctor, starting his sentence with the same informal words he always used. "Your job can be physically and mentally taxing and the boss wants to know you are in good condition. Now, please lower your pants and pull your shorts to your knees. Cough please, and turn your head."

A mental note had been taken that Eddie was not circumcised. Also, he had an ugly tattoo on his bicep. When the doctor placed a surgical glove on his hand, Eddie let out a sigh.

"Hey doc, I'm not an astronaut," he complained.

In a moment the ordeal was over. The doctor pricked Eddie's finger and drew some blood, picked up his urine sample and left the room. Eddie quickly dressed and walked out the now vacant front office. He could hear the whinny from a horse in the corral below and the lights in the kitchen of the mansion burned brightly.

"Man, oh man, what a day," he sighed, as he climbed into his Chevy and drove down the long driveway to the highway.

Inside the mansion, a smiling man watched the tail lights, as Eddie turned right. He slapped Jerry on the back, as a van also turned right, stopping momentarily at the mansion's gates.

"Just remember, man, there's no way in hell that guy's goin' to wear my costumes," said E., as he walked back from his bedroom window.

Eddie never noticed the van that was following him. His spirits were soaring and he needed a drink. He had costume fittings scheduled for tomorrow afternoon and he still needed to let K-Mart know that he wouldn't be returning. Strutting into "The Robin's Nest", he felt like the man. The D.J. was announcing a Karaoke contest. Eddie sneered as he looked around the dingy club and thought of performing in front of all these poor drunks. Then, smiling to himself, he raised his hand and entered the contest. A large black woman, an elderly blonde, in sequined pants, her blouse tied tightly under her sagging breasts and a lean cowboy with a baby face also raised their hands.

"Well folks, so far we have four contestants, who's first?" asked the D.J.

The black woman raised her massive arm and sauntered up to the mike. She performed a rendition of "Respect" that brought the house down. She jiggled. She twisted. She squatted. People parking outside came in just to hear Marquetta Julliet do her thing. Not really an amateur, Marquetta just couldn't stay sober long enough to last in a band.

"Wow, that was great! How about you blondie?" yelled the D.J.

She chugged down her beer, climbed on stage and sang an old Dolly Parton song, "Here We Go Again."

The D.J. reminded Eddie of the guy on the "Gong Show". The blonde was awful and with all the expressions the D.J. was making, he told everyone that he thought she better keep her day job. Finally, she finished.

"Hey cowboy, you ready?" he yelled.

"Ya, I guess so. Can I play my guitar?" the cowboy asked.

"Sure, go ahead," yelled the D.J., trying to keep the audience's enthusasm up.

Eddie whirled around in his chair as the young cowboy sang "Jailhouse Rock", driving the audience wild as he danced across the floor. He ended the number by saying, "Thank-you, thank-you very much."

The prize for the evening was a fifty dollar gift certificate to Western World, but this didn't seem to matter to Eddie anymore. He raised his hand, walked up to the mike and told the D.J. to put on "American Trilogy."

"We ain't got that, man," said the D.J., looking through his records and tapes.

Eddie looked behind him, puzzled. Two men were standing up at their table, at the far side of the bar. They motioned to him, beckoning Eddie to join them.

"Sorry man," said the D.J., as Eddie left the stage and walked towards the two men.

Cheers went up from the Karaoke crowd, as the young cowboy picked up his certificate.

Eddie couldn't help but swallow hard, as these two guys smiled at him. They reminded him of the F.B.I. guys who had removed his manager from the first K-Mart store he had worked in.

"Hi, Mr. Arroyo, sit down. Can we buy you a drink," the heavy-set thug said, extending his hand towards Eddie.

"Who the hell are you guys?" asked Eddie, not offering his hand-shake.

"Eddie, we are with private security," they replied as they flashed two plastic identification cards at him, magically slipping them back into their starched, military-pressed shirts.

Eddie started to laugh. "You guys are shittin' me, right?"

"Mr. Arroyo, may I remind you that you are now an employee of the company."

The conversation stopped, as the waitress delivered three drinks, all cokes, to their table.

"Do you understand that you are on probation?" continued the heavy-set man.

"Well, yes. But, I didn't do nuthin' wrong," barked Eddie.

The younger of the two men kept his head down. But, his deep, green eyes bore into Eddie's eyes. He never said a word.

"Let's look at it this way. Would E. come in this place?"

Eddie thought about this for a minutes, finally agreeing that he probably wouldn't be caught dead the "The Robin's Nest."

"But, then again, I'm not him," he said, pushing his chair back from the table and rising to his feet.

The young detective stood up at the same time.

"Sit down, Mr. Arroyo. We're here to prevent you from getting into any embarrassing situations. Consider that your actions not only reflect on the company, they also reflect on your employer.

Eddie slowly lowered his large body back into the chair. He felt like he had been busted. But, he didn't know for what. Thinking back on his K-Mart training, he mentally made a decision to take charge of this situation. He took a deep breath and a large drink of his coke. Eddie balled up his fist. Then, as he started to talk, an explosion in his head stopped his thoughts. Red and yellow streamers, he was drowning a deep, black cloud. Slowly, his head fell forward onto the table. Eddie Arroyo was asleep. Customers and staff of "The Robin's Nest" didn't even notice. They had become accustomed to drunks being carried out of the bar. The only person who gave Eddie a second glance was the waitress who had served the non-alcoholic cokes. But, when she saw the ten dollar bill on the table, she stuck it in her pocket and went on to the next customers who were yelling at her for a drink. If two men were carrying their buddy out the door of this dive, she wasn't going to ask any questions.

Shards of light cut deeply into Eddie's cornea, as he turned over in bed. The sky light above the bed, the cool air conditioning blowing on him, all seemed strange. It took Eddie's mind a few seconds to register the reality of his situation. He wasn't in his apartment.

"What the hell is goin' on?" he said, sitting on the edge of the bed, holding his aching head with his large hands.

He had to go to the bathroom. Noticing that his clothes were missing, he pulled down his boxer shorts and sat down on the commode. The bathroom was white and as sterile as a hospital. This thought scared him. As he slowly walked back into the bedroom, a sharp knock startled him.

"Mr. Arroyo, Mr. Arroyo?" heralded the voice.

"Ya man, what's goin' on? Unlock this damn door and get me outa here," Eddie yelled, twisting the door knob.

"Put your clothes on. They are in the closet, next to the bathroom," said the mystery man, as Eddie heard his footsteps disappear from the door.

Spotting a phone on the dresser, Eddie picked up the receiver and began dialing the operator. Disgusted, he slammed the phone down. All the lights were lit across the bottom of the phone. All the lines were in use and Eddie couldn't get a dial tone. He pounded on the door and screamed obscene words. His head ached. Sitting on the edge of the bed again, he heard a strange noise. It sounded like someone was bouncing a basketball on a wooden floor.

"Where the hell am I," he screamed.

Slipping the blue jogging-suit and Rockport tennis shoes on, he tried the door once more. This time the door opened. Stepping out the door, he cautiously looked both ways and approached the metal railing of the balcony he was standing on. Looking over the balcony, his eyes opened wide. He was in the racketball area of the mansion.

Eddie was in his gym. He had spent the night sleeping above this legend's racketball court and Eddie didn't know how he had gotten there. All he could remember was "The Robin's Nest" and the two men that had threatened him. As he looked down at his strange blue jogging-suit, he wondered if it belonged to him. Running his hand through his hair, he walked down the winding staircase. This whole thing was way too weird. He was going to find out just what was going on. At this moment, Eddie Arroyo had just about all the show business life he ever wanted and he was planning on giving it right back to the mansion.

Stepping off the last carpeted step, he was greeted by applause. Marlene and Dr. Someti raised their wine glasses and toasted him. Dr. Someti slapped Eddie on the back, saying that he sure looked like the man walking down those stairs. Before Eddie could question last night's kidnapping, Marlene popped the cork on another bottle of Dom and poured him a large glass. Grabbing Eddie's large arm she led him from the gym back to the main house. Eddie glanced at the beautiful grounds as he followed her into the back door.

The cook was in the kitchen and the smell of fresh bread, bacon, eggs and coffee made Eddie's mouth water. Marlene led Eddie up the stairs.

"Please Eddie, sit down and have some breakfast," she said, motioning him towards a huge buffet table.

The table was laden with eggs, bacon, sausage, muffins, éclairs, fruit, doughnuts, grits, fried potatoes and coffee. Eddie filled his plate to the top. As he sat down in a large fur covered chair, he realized that he was in another famous room in the mansion.

"Eddie, man-oh-man, you sure tied one on last night," said one of the security men, taking a big bite out of his jelly doughnut.

"I never had a drink, except that coke you guys bought me!" replied Eddie, setting his plate down on the footstool and standing up.

"Oh shit, look out, he's mad," said the green-eyed security man.

Everyone burst out laughing, falling over on their sides, while Eddie, his face red with anger, stood in the middle of the room staring at them. Everyone knew what was going on, except Eddie, and he didn't like the feelings that were stirring inside of him.

"What's so damn funny?"

"Eddie, relax. Have your breakfast and keep an open mind about our actions," said Marlene, taking a sip of her coffee.

"No, no way. I want an explanation. Why was I drugged and kidnapped?"

"Eddie, those are some pretty strong words. Keep an open mind. You were in a bad place. "The Robin's Nest" is owned by the Belusi brothers. They are into all kinds of ugly stuff; prostitution, narcotics, child porn. We are only looking out for your best interests. We're here to protect you," said the fat security guard.

"That's right, E. is sick, Mr. Arroyo. We need you and your talents to help him or he will be dead in six months. He must go to Hong Kong for treatment, then Switzerland for a cure and finally to an undisclosed treatment facility for his much needed rest," said the green-eyed guard.

Eddie, his anger draining from him at the thought of his idol dying, sat quietly in the chair and nodded his head in agreement. A maid was clearing the table and breakfast was officially over. No one moved. A moment of silence came over the room. Marlene was the first to speak.

"Eddie, let's go outside."

Slowly the entire group moved outside the mansion and walked past the pool to the meditation garden, a spot where they often sat and contemplated the day's events. Marlene wiped her eyes as she told Eddie about the large costume belt that E. wore for his performances.

"It's covering a tube, Eddie. This tube is called a drain tube and it's only a temporary cure until we can find a new liver for him. Will you help us, please?" Marlene cried, wiping her eyes and putting her arms around his neck.

Her perfume saturated his mind. Her knee pressed against his thigh and at this moment he would have killed anyone, jumped off anything, or said whatever they wanted. After all, he was their super-hero. All thoughts or questions about their actions flew from his mind, shelved far away from his common sense.

"I understand," he heard himself saying. "What do you want me to do?"

"Just be him until he's well. You will be preserving a great national treasure. Otherwise, it may wither away," she answered.

Eddie heard himself saying, "I'll do it darlin', anything you need."

Dr. Someti, who had been quiet, spoke next.

"The tattoo will have to go," he said, pointing at Eddie's dragon and lady proudly displayed on his bicep.

"Well, that's one I didn't expect," laughed Eddie, running his hand over his tattoo.

"I know you have business to attend to today, so please be at my office in Southhaven tonight at eleven-thirty. This is the address. It's not far from here," said Dr. Someti.

Eddie took the slip of paper from the doctor and slipped it in his shirt pocket. Looking at his watch, he realized that he had not called K-

Mart and he had a costume fitting in Collierville in two hours.

"Look, I'm runnin' a little behind, so I'm goin' to go. I'll be at home later this afternoon if ya need me. Y'all know I'm ready to do whatever ya want. Right?"

Marlene looked at Eddie and smiled. She knew he would do whatever they wanted.

At eleven-fifteen Eddie pulled into the dark parking lot of a small office building. He checked the address against his paper and was sure that this was the place. As he walked past the high hedges to the front door, the hair on his neck bristled. Brushing the eerie feeling away, he knocked on the door. Dr. Someti opened the door and greeted him with his usual, "Well Eddie, are you ready?"

"Doc, are ya sure we gotta go through this? I mean, no one is gonna see the tattoo on stage."

"Well Eddie, just relax and it will be over in a few minutes."

Eddie felt the injection into his arm and winced. Then his arm went totally numb. He closed his eyes and slipped into a drug induced sleep. Dr. Someti deftly, surgically removed the offending tattoo of a dragon wrapped around a voluptuous, screaming lady. An hour later, Eddie stared at his swollen and bandaged arm. Pulling back the bandage, he was horrified to see the large open wound that looked like he had been hacked apart with a steak knife. Dr. Someti replaced the bandage and assured him that with a skin graph, he would look like he had never had a tattoo. He gave Eddie one hundred pain pills and a bottle of antibiotics and told him to go home and sleep.

    The next morning, his arm burning and throbbing, he pulled the soaked bandage from his tender skin. The deep crescent cut, the color of watermelon, seemed to be on fire. He swallowed the two pain pills and drifted to sleep, picturing himself on stage. The best groups were singing back-up, flash-bulbs exploded in his eyes and the crowd stood, filling auditorium with thunderous applause. As he finished "American Trilogy", his arms raised to God, he knew he was the new king.

A few hours later, his bed covered with smears of blood and his arm feeling like it had been hit by a sledge-hammer, Eddie staggered to the phone. He asked information for the doctor's number and swore at the operator when she informed him that she had no listing for a Dr. Someti in Southhaven or Memphis. The next call was placed to the offices of the mansion.

"Good afternoon, thank you for calling. Please, stay on the line and the operator will assist you."

Mellow ballads filtered through the phone lines, while Eddie fumed. He wasn't feeling good enough for this run-around.

"Hello, good-afternoon. How may I direct your call?"

"Get me Marlene Hardison, this is Eddie Arroyo," he yelled.

"One moment, Mr. Arroyo."

More music poured into his already throbbing head. A few seconds later Marlene answered the phone.

"Yes Eddie, may I help you?" said Marlene, very business-like.

"I need Dr. Someti's number. My damn arm is falling off."

"I am so sorry, Eddie. I will have the doctor call you."

"But, I want his number," he said, as Marlene hung up the phone. She giggled to herself. At least he had a hill-billy pecker or he would also have a new schmuck.

Swearing, Eddie turned on the television. "Wild Adventure" was on. Elephants, tigers and African landscape moved across the screen. Eddie watched, hoping to take his mind off the pain in his arm. A loud knock at the door shook him back to reality.

"Come in man, my arm's on fire," Eddie said as the doctor walked into his small, stuffy apartment.

The doctor peeled back the bandage and looked at the crescent scar.

"Well Eddie, looks like we have a nasty infection here. I'm going to take you to Baptist for treatment."

Eddie watched, as the doctor called the hospital and told them he was admitting a patient. Today, Dr. Someti looked very strange to Eddie. He was dressed in a slogan tee shirt and Levis. On his feet were penny-loafers.

"Hey doc, where did you get those shoes?" Eddie asked, feeling some relief from the pain shot the doctor had administered.

The doctor ignored Eddie's question. He was busy cleaning the wound and bandaging Eddie's arm.

"Well Eddie, I think while you are in the hospital, it would be a good time to get the rest of the work done, don't you?"

Eddie pulled his swollen arm away from the doctor and turned to face him. "What are you talking about, man?"

"Well Eddie, as you know E. is very ill. You agreed to help. Well Eddie, that's where the bonus starts kicking in. You get $8,000 a month, plus $10,000 cash after the surgery is completed."

Eddie's mind reeled at the $10,000 figure. The morphine the doctor had given him made his head fuzzy. Thoughts of an air-conditioned apartment, new car, fancy clothes and fame swam through his mind.

"What kind of surgery are y'all talkin' about?"

"Well, the lips are wrong. You can't sneer with those lips. Nose needs some work and E. has blue eyes, contacts will do the job there."

"Will I look like him, when ya get done, man?"

"Well Eddie, we have a plastic surgeon, in L.A. He works on the stars; Dina, Cher, Burt and now Eddie Arroyo. Yes, it will work. No one will know that you are not the real thing.

"Will he see me?"

"Well, you see he isn't to be bothered with this. He needs his rest. But, he can't rest until you are ready. That means his; songs, clothes, speech, friend's names and memories must be mastered by you. This pays another $20,000. Let's run over this again, Eddie. You will get $8,000 a month, $10,000 cash after the surgery, $20,000 for the make-over and memory course. Sound's good, doesn't it? Your employers are very generous. But, you have to be willing to carry it off. You must be better than ever. What do you think? Do you have the balls to handle your job?"

"Ya, I guess so man. But, my arm won't quit bleedin'," replied Eddie, looking at the crimson bandage on his bicep.

"Well Eddie, I promise you, when they get finished with you at Baptist, you will feel like a new man. Now, let's go."

The trip to the hospital was uneventful. Dr. Someti pulled his Cadillac around to the service entrance and parked by a door marked private. Entering a service elevator, they arrived on the eighth floor. The wind reserved for Eddie contained four large suites. The doors were tightly closed to the suites and the hallway was deserted. His suite had a living room, bedroom and bathroom. It was tastefully decorated and had fresh flowers on the table by the window.

"Wow, is this a hospital or a hotel?" said Eddie, flopping down on the white leather couch in front of the large television.

"Well Eddie, this is a special suite reserved for celebrities. You will not have any unauthorized visitors or phone calls. Your nurses are all private duty and you are not to leave this suite. Do you understand? We must not arouse any suspicion over your make-over."

"Gosh, I feel like a star. Is this the room that he used when he was in Baptist?"

"Eddie, that is confidential. But, you should probably lie down. The pills I have given you will relax you and you should sleep. The plastic surgeon will be in to see you later."

Eddie stretched out on the couch and turned on the T.V. He closed his eyes.

"Ya, this is the king's room. I'm in the king's room," he thought, as he drifted into a light sleep.

Around six, Eddie awoke to a light knock on his hospital door. A nurse entered the room with a tray of wonderful smelling food. She arranged his table by the window with the steaming dishes and asked him if there was anything he needed.

"Darlin', do you have any pain medication? My arm is throbbing, again."

"Of course, Mr. Summers, I will bring you something," she said.

"Mr. Summers? What the hell is goin on?" thought Eddie, finally realizing that he was using an alias.

Eddie was almost through with his large steak and baked potato when the nurse entered the room. She asked him to remove his clothes and slip into special hospital pajamas. Eddie thought about the usual backless hospital gowns the regular people get and smiled. His pajamas were of fine silk and his terry robe was so soft that you could use if for a blanket.

"Got my shot," asked Eddie.

"Yes, Mr. Summers. Please drop your pajamas bottoms down and relax."

Eddie turned around, while the nurse shot him in the left cheek. She was so good, that he didn't even feel the shot. After his dessert, he climbed into bed and turned on the other T.V., suspended in front of his bed. The news was just ending, when the plastic surgeon opened the hospital room door.

"Mr. Summers, I am Dr. Nudgent. I will be performing your cosmetic surgery. We will be doing the surgery early in the morning. So, no food or drink after midnight. Now, if you will relax and lay back on the bed, I would like to do my preliminary work. I have the results of all the tests that Dr. Someti ran on you, so there will be little lab work needed. We will be doing a little Rhinoplasty and a little cosmetic surgery in the area of your lips. There will be minor discomfort and bruising."

"Hey doc, while you're here, can you look at my arm. Dr. Someti removed my tattoo and I can't get it to stop bleedin'."

The doctor removed the bandage and stared at the large, angry scar.

"Did you say that he removed a tattoo? It appears that you have a large open scar here. I would like to do some cosmetic surgery on it, at a later date, otherwise you are going to be left with a large half-moon shaped scar on your upper arm. I will have the nurse apply some topical antibiotic and bandage. But, I feel that you should talk to your doctor about having a skin graph."

Eddie listened to the plastic surgeon, remembering that Dr. Someti mentioned something about skin graphs. The pain medication was working, so he pushed the thought of future surgery from his mind. About an hour later the doctor was finished with his work and the nurse brought Eddie a sleeping pill. He turned on the T.V. again, and soon was asleep.

As they wheeled him into a surgical theater, Eddie asked the doctor if he would be O.K. He had signed surgery releases the night before and he worried. The doctor assured him that he would be fine. The last thing Eddie remembered was the bright light above his head. It looked like a spot-light. Eddie thought he was on stage at the Hilton, in Lake Tahoe.

Eddie woke up again to pain. But, this time it was his face that throbbed. He reached for his call button and a nurse appeared magically at his side.

"Mr. Summers, you're awake. How are you feeling?"

Eddie tried to talk, but the bandages on his mouth prevented him from speaking clearly. The nurse seemed to understand. She administered a shot and Eddie drifted.

Dr. Nudgent checked on him later in the day and said that he would be released in a day or two, as soon as the drain could be removed. He assured Eddie that he would heal beautifully. That was the last time Eddie saw Dr. Nudgent. The nurses, however, never left him alone. They were constantly checking his bandages, giving him back-rubs and feeding him wonderful food by spoon or straw. On the second day, Dr. Someti removed the bandages from Eddie's face and replaced them with smaller bandaging over his nose. He was swollen and sore, but couldn't find a mirror in his room to see how he looked. He also removed the drains.

"Darlin, do you have a mirror?" Eddie asked one of the nurses.

"Mr. Summers, you are not allowed to view your reconstructive surgery. The doctor would have our heads if we brought you a mirror. But, except for some swelling and bruising, you look wonderful," she said.   "In fact, has anyone ever told you that you look a lot like another famous person who lives in Memphis?"

Eddie felt his breath catch in his chest. He gingerly touched his bandages and closed his eyes.

"I'm the luckiest son-of-a-bitch on this planet," he thought.

The next morning the rumor had spread through the hospital that someone resembling the king, was on the eighth floor. Nurses and orderlies, out of their jurisdiction, made quick stops by Eddie's room. One nurse even asked him if he was the man. Eddie, trying his best to handle the attention, denied her suspicions.

"Darlin," drawled Eddie, trying to sound like his idol, "you sure are pretty. But, you got it all wrong. I'm Mr. Summers."

The nurse blushed a deep shade of red and backed out of Eddie's room. She was sure it was him.

Dr. Someti showed up right after Eddie's breakfast. Closing the curtain around his bed, he examined Eddie's face and smiled.

"Well Eddie, let's get out of here."

As Eddie dressed, he noticed that several men were stationed in the hall outside his room. A nurse came in with a wheel chair and told him to get in it. She wheeled him through the door, where she was replaced by four of the mansion's security.

"Hey guys, it's good to see ya," said Eddie.

"Hold the talk till we're free of this place," said Jerry.

Eddie shut his mouth and allowed them to wheel him to the service elevator and out the back door. A white limo waited at the curb. Just as Eddie moved from the chair to the car, a security guard's camera flashed in his face. One of the men with Eddie, his teeth clenched in rage, grabbed the camera from the guard, smashing it to the pavement.

Eddie stared at the guard's pale face, as Jerry ripped the film from the camera. Pushing his way in next to Eddie, he told the driver to go. Within seconds, the Limo was on the expressway, heading towards his apartment.

"Betcha that asshole is picking up his nineteen dollar camera, worrying about where he is going to collect his next pay check," said Jerry, as he unrolled the offending film.

"Hey Eddie, talkin about money, I guess you're goin to be a lot richer when you get home," laughed the big man who had smashed the camera.

"Ya, I guess," replied Eddie, fingering the bandage on his face.

Marlene greeted the bandaged pretender, as Eddie walked into his apartment. It was torture for him not to rip the bandages from his face. He excused himself and went to the bathroom. Staring at his reflection in the mirror, he couldn't see much of a change. Dr. Someti had added more bandages and he could see his eyes and swollen lips, but not much more. As he came out of the bathroom, Marlene introduced him to a young black woman in a starched nurse's uniform.

"What's with the bedpan woman," Eddie whispered, as he hugged Marlene.

Marlene laughed. "She's a nurse's assistant and her name is Virginia. She'll be here days, keeping an eye on your arm and face. She's got the pain shots Eddie, so treat her nice."

"When do the bandages come off my face?"

"Approximately two weeks," answered Virginia. "Can I get you anything?"

"No, just leave me alone," Eddie said, walking towards his bedroom. He looked at Marlene, ran his hands over his bandaged face and closed the door.

A few days later, Dr. Someti told Eddie that his face was healing nicely.

"Doc, let me see it," asked Eddie.

"Well Eddie, I think it would be best if we waited a few more days," he replied, as he placed the bandages across his face. "But, I'm going to discontinue the pain shots. Virginia has pain pills for you, if you need them."

Virginia had reported that Eddie was eating well and drinking beer. The seemed unconcerned.

Eddie had a hard time getting off the pain shots. He fought with Virginia, but she had her orders. So Eddie took the two pain pills she gave him and washed them down with a beer. That seemed to work. He was up and feeling good.

Seven days had passed since the surgery, as Eddie stepped out of the shower he couldn't resist the temptation any longer. Carefully pulling the bandages from his face, he shut his eyes tight. As the last bandage dropped to the floor, he opened them and stared at his image in the full-length mirror. The reflection in the mirror startled him. In fact, it would have startled most people. It was the image of a naked E. with a slightly bruised face and a swollen lip. Letting his fingers graze over his new features, he found himself becoming aroused at his own reflection.

"Mother of God, I am the king."

"Mr. Arroyo, are you all right?" said Virginia, knocking lightly on the door.

"Damn, I did it," yelled Eddie.

The door knob clicked. The door swung wide. Virginia's mouth dropped open, as a nude Eddie growled with his arms straight out in front of him. Still somewhat aroused, he chased this frightened nurse's assistant around the apartment. Virginia ran into the living room, falling over the edge of the coffee table. Eddie made a quick right turn and cut her off in the hall. Screaming she ran through the kitchen and towards the front door. Grabbing her keys off the hook, she ran down the steps and straight to her car. Laughing hysterically, Eddie watched her Toyota burn rubber as she drove wildly out of the apartment complex, leaving her purse, medical bag, paperwork and medications on the couch. Finally composing himself, Eddie posed in the mirror, while slipping on his shorts. The crescent slice on his arm was now a salmon color and still remained sore. But, Eddie didn't care.

Finally dressed, he took his pain pills with a beer and answered the door. A Federal Express delivery man stood at the door, an envelope in his hand. As Eddie signed for his delivery, the young man stared at Eddie. Finally, he said something.

"Hey man, anyone ever tell you that you look like that rock and roll singer?"

"You mean the king?" Eddie answered.

"Ya, that's the guy?"

"No," Eddie said, grabbing the envelope and closing the door.

Uncontrolled laughter rolled from Eddie's mouth as he opened the envelope. Ten crisp thousand dollar bills tumbled out on the floor. Kneeling and finally falling completely down on the floor, he threw himself on the money. Rolling on his back, he sang the words to "Caught In A Trap" as loud as he could sing.

CHAPTER THREE

Virginia wasted no time in calling Marlene. She would have called the cops but, she wanted to get her pay check first.

"Miss Hardison, why he's plum crazy. He done attacked me and lord knows what he was goin to do's to me. I ain't never seen a more lustful man. You can't pay me enough to go back in that place."

Marlene smoked two cigarettes and cursed silently under her breath, as she listened to the whole bizarre story.

"I apologize for Mr. Arroyo's behavior. Will an extra bonus in your envelope help you get over this awful experience?" asked Marlene.

"Well . . . I was jus about to call the cops. But, you is bein so good about my feelins. That man's also got my purse," cried Virginia.

Marlene visibly paled at the mention of the police.

"Virginia, I will get your purse and anything that you left at the apartment. You come by my office tomorrow afternoon and I'm sure we can work this whole thing out. O.K.?"

"Yes, Miss Hardison. Thanks for bein so understandin," replied a somewhat calmer Virginia.

Marlene hung up the phone and slammed her fist on the desk.

"Tammy, get me Someti on the phone, now!" yelled Marlene.

"Hey doc, we got a problem. Eddie has ripped the bandages from his face and is acting very strange. Get over there as soon as you can. I don't want that fool screwing everything up."

Dr. Someti asked about Virginia and sighed as Marlene recapped the event.

"Sounds to me like the surgery was a success. Send some men over there to keep an eye on him, before this guy tries out his new face on the locals. Have them take care of the loose ends with Virginia, too," ordered Dr. Someti.

"I've got it covered, doc. You just get over there and let me know what's up."

Eddie picked up the money from the floor and stuffed it in his pocket. He was so excited. Pacing around the apartment, he grabbed his car keys from the hook by the door and looked at his reflection one more time in the mirror.

"Time for me to get some new threads. E. shops on Beale, so Eddie shops on Beale," he sang to himself, as he opened the front door to his apartment.

"God doc, you startled me," said Eddie, staring at the doctor who stood in his doorway.

"Going somewhere, Eddie?" asked the doctor, as he backed Eddie into the apartment and closed the door.

Looking down at the keys in his hand, Eddie told the doctor that he was just going to run down to the convenience store for some beer.

"Well Eddie, I don't think that would be such a good idea. I see you have removed your bandages. Step over here in the light and let me look at your face."

"Doc, I look great. That guy you sent did a job on me. Man, I look like him. Don't you think?"

Dr. Someti didn't answer Eddie. He poked around on his face and took a needle from his case.

"Roll up your sleeve. This will prevent any infection. You are healing nicely. But, the sun can cause scaring to the tissue. You must stay in the apartment until the bruising disappears."

"Man, I'm going crazy in this place. You gotta let me get outa here for a spell," complained Eddie.

Dr. Someti reached his hand in his pocket and fingered the snub nose revolver.

"Eddie, sit down on the couch and relax. Marlene will be here soon and I'm sure we can work something out."

Eddie felt weak in his legs. He lowered his body to the couch. The shot was taking effect. As Eddie closed his eyes, the doctor picked up the phone and called Marlene.

"Dr. Someti, put Marlene on the phone."

"Ya doc, any problems?"

"Eddie's going to need a guard and I've taken his car keys. Get over here as soon as you can and bring some beer. I don't know what kind. Something cheap."

"I'm on it. How's the face?"

"My employer would be proud," said the doctor looking at the handsome man asleep on the couch.

Marlene smiled when she thought about her boss and the money she was getting. The smile slipped from her face as she picked up her purse and placed a quick call to Audrey.

"Hi darling, I'm going to be late. The S.O.B. is acting up and I've got to go babysit. Don't hold dinner," she said into the answering service.

Dr. Someti walked out on the landing of Eddie's upstairs apartment. The black Cadillac was parked in the first parking spot across from Eddie's apartment door. The man in the car turned on their lights briefly, signaling their presence. Sighing deeply, a tired doctor opened the apartment door and walked back into the living room. Eddie had fallen over on his side. The doctor pulled a pillow off the bed and placed it under Eddie's head.

"No use getting any creases in that fine face of yours," he thought.

Marlene arrived at Eddie's apartment several hours later. Eddie was still on the couch. His eyes were closed. Dr. Someti was dozing in the green vinyl recliner.

"Looks like I was really needed," Marlene said sarcastically.

"Well Marlene, you finally got here. Looks like our boy is still out cold. The shot must have done the trick. I think we should move him out to the club, don't you? That way we can keep a better eye on him and avoid any ugly problems."

Eddie listened to the doctor and a cold feeling came over him. He was still groggy from the shot. But, not too groggy to figure out he was in danger.

Marlene walked into the kitchen and put a six-pack in the refrigerator. "I think he will be O.K. tonight and I've still got that Virginia mess to worry about. You go on. I'm going to collect her things and clean up anything that may have been hers. Eddie looks to me like he's out for the night."

Dr. Someti picked up his bag and left. A half-hour later, Marlene left with all of Virginia's possessions. Eddie slowly opened his eyes and sat up on the couch.

"What the hell is going on here? I must have been dreamin. If I was a prisoner, they'd still be here," thought Eddie, as he opened the refrigerator and took a can of beer from the six-pack Marlene had picked up.

"Dixie Beer, great. Now, if I just had a pizza to go with this," said Eddie, as he picked up the phone and ordered a large sausage and cheese.

Eddie sat back down on the couch and popped open his beer. Switching on the late news, he listened to the usual stuff, an apartment fire, a convenience store robbery and a family dispute, ending in stabbing. His mind wandered. An accident on 3rd Street caught his attention. A nurse, Virginia Holms, had been killed when her Toyota suddenly burst into flames, causing her to veer into the path of an eighteen wheeler. The driver of the truck was uninjured. He said that she had pulled away from the curb and into traffic. Then for no reason, her car exploded, throwing her into his path. The accident is under investigation.

"Shit, the bed-pan lady fried herself. That's weird. Here today, gone tomorrow," said Eddie, as he looked out the window for the pizza-man.

Eddie noticed that a large Cadillac was now blocking the drive-way.

"What the hell?"

Mastos's Pizza Delivery stopped abruptly, waiting for the Caddy to move. Instead, a man got out of the car and walked up to the pizza truck. In a minute, the man had the pizza and the delivery person was gone. He was walking up the steps to Eddie's apartment.

"Man, I'm not openin the door. It's probably a drug deal and I'll get busted," said Eddie, as he sat back down on the couch in the living room. "I ain't goin to let him in. He can eat that damn thing himself," he said, as the man knocked loudly on the door.

Eventually the locked door suddenly clicked open, Eddie stared at an Al Capone character standing in the doorway, holding the pizza box. The man moved his considerable bulk into the kitchen and sat the pizza on the kitchen table. Eddie stood up from the couch and clenched his fists.

"It's paid for," said the man, turning on his heel and slamming the door on the way out of the apartment.

Eddie flipped back the lid of the pizza box. The aroma of a fresh, hot pizza filled the kitchen.

"I'm not friggin goin to take this shit," yelled Eddie, as he dialed Marlene's private number.

"Listen Marlene, remove the thug character from in front of the apartment. I'm goin out to see my girl and I'll beat the shit outa anyone who stops me," he yelled, as her answering service came on.

Marlene heard the message, as she sat in the quiet darkness of her office. The grounds of the mansion seemed strangely vacant with her boss away. Lighting a cigarette, she picked up Eddie's file. Flipping to the page marked personal family and close relationships, she came across the name Janet Macary, PPC. Stationed at Millington, female-lover.

Eddie paced around the kitchen, eating the pizza and wondering what he could do about his situation. The car keys weren't hanging on the hook and his face was aching. He finished the pizza and grabbed his fifth beer. Slugging down three pain pills he went into the bathroom. His reflection in the medicine cabinet mirror caught his attention. He couldn't help staring at the face, his face. Smiling to himself, he went into the bedroom, laid down on the bed and thought about his upcoming performance.

"Man, get yourself together. You got it all, money, the face and a chance to perform.

Don't screw it up or you'll be back at K-Mart," he said to himself, closing his eyes.

The next morning, Marlene placed a call to Eddie.

"Yah," Eddie answered, rubbing his eyes and stretching.

"Hi, big boy?"

"Who's this," asked Eddie.

"Who do you want it to be, you big stud," replied Marlene, laughing.

Eddie couldn't answer. He was sure it was Marlene. But, she didn't sound like the Marlene he knew.

"I have some great news for you. We're going out. Guess where?"

"Marlene, is that you?"

"How about it, burning love? You and I at the Peabody?"

"God, yes, I mean that would be great. I'm going crazy in this dump," said Eddie.

"I'll send doc over with some new clothes this afternoon. You rest up and we will turn this town upside-down tonight, baby," said Marlene.

"Great Miss Hardison, I mean Marlene. You bet, I'll see you tonight. Thanks."

Marlene hung up the phone, swearing at her rotten job. This morning Audrey had pushed her away and told her she spend too much time at work. Now, this!

Her next phone call was to Someti. She lit another cigarette and took a drink of her cold coffee.

"Hey doc, this is Marlene. Guess what, Eddie wants the guards removed and he wants to see his girl. Yah, he has a girlfriend. It was right here in the report. We must have over-looked it. This could ruin everything. I got him calmed down, for now. But, can you imagine them going out together? The press would be on him like hot butter on flap-jacks. Call the Balushi brothers, do something!"

"Hey sweet-cheeks, calm down. Every mission has problems. When I was in the Big One, World War Two . . ."

Dr. Someti heard the phone slam down and knew Marlene didn't appreciate being called sweet-cheeks.

Dr. Someti waited until afternoon to arrive at Eddie's apartment. According to the guards that had watched his apartment, everyone had gone to work and the place would be empty. He was sure that Eddie was getting suspicious of his sedative injections, so this time it would be a little harder to knock Eddie out. He stopped at the doughnut shop on the way to the apartment and bought a dozen doughnuts. Injecting the shot into the doughnut was easy. Now, all he had to do was get Eddie to eat the right one.

Eddie smiled a big smile when he heard the knock on the door.

"Just a second, Marlene," he called.

"Well Eddie, I'm sorry to disappoint you, but it's not Marlene."

"Oh, hi doc. I thought you were Miss Hardison."

"I heard about your date Eddie. Nice moves."

"Hey doc, she asked me."

Dr. Someti examined Eddie's face and then stood back about a foot from the imposter's features.

"Yes, yes, I do believe that you could fool the king himself. Now, roll up your sleeve and let me see your arm."

"Listen doc, no more shots. They make me feel funny. Don't want anything to screw up my date tonight."

"O.K. Eddie, no more shots. You hungry? There's doughnuts on the counter. The jelly ones are E.'s favorite."

Eddie opened the box and looked at the variety. In the center was a large jelly doughnut. Picking it up with his large hand, he took a big bite.

"I can see why he likes these. You should've gotten more than one jelly doughnut or did you eat some?"

"Whoops, you caught me. A habit from my childhood. My mother didn't let us kids have sweets, so the first job I held when I went to college was in a doughnut shop. Still can't get enough of them."

Eddie finished the doughnut and licked his fingers.

"Marlene said you were goin to bring me some new threads to wear tonight for our dinner at the Peabody. Where are they?"

"Well, your arm looks fine and your face is healing. I left the clothes at the mansion. We are going to drive over there and try them on. So Eddie, let's go."

Eddie's head felt a little light as he walked down the stairs to the doctor's car. By the time they pulled out on Winchester, Eddie was slumped against the door, unconscious. The tinted windows of the doctor's car protected

Eddie's face from the sun and kept out the spying eyes of other motorists. Within minutes, Eddie Arroyo's limp body was deposited on the bed in the room above the racketball court. Tony stood outside the locked door and the phone lines had been cut to Eddie's new room. Tonight, Eddie Arroyo would die.

CHAPTER FOUR

It had taken the Balushi brothers four days to find a derelict who resembled Eddie. Waiting outside Memphis Mental Health, they had seen more strange characters wander in and out of that place then they thought possible. This guy seemed perfect. He was six foot tall, over two hundred pounds and had no identification on him. By the looks of his clothes and the way he smelled, they were sure he was a homeless drunk. Enticing him with a bottle of brandy, laced with a heavy drug, was easy. The rest was just a matter of planning.

Eddie slept all through the day, unaware that an explosion had ripped through his apartment, leveling his home and the adjoining apartment. The police and fire department agreed that the unfortunate death of Eddie Arroyo was the result of a gas leak in the kitchen area. Suicide was considered, then ruled out. The coroner officially listed the death as accidental.

Dr. Someti watched the scene from a safe distance. He felt a sense of relief and sadness, as the coroner hauled the body from the rubble and placed it in the ambulance. People milled around the apartment complex, shooting pictures of the giant hole in the front of the apartment building and talking to the news media. The mood was almost festive, as the police strung the yellow crime-scene tape across the front of the crumbling stairs. Again, the doctor thought about the destruction he had witnessed during the war.

"Another mission accomplished," he said, as he pulled past the police cars and headed back to the mansion.

Eddie's face was all over the news by evening. The landlord of the apartment building had positively identified the body. His ex-boss from K-Mart gave a touching interview about what a good employee he had been and the mansion was unavailable for comment.

Janet Macary heard the news as she was eating dinner in the mess hall. Shocked, she tried to call Eddie's apartment. Listening to the funny ringing of an out-of-order phone line, tears rolled down her cheeks. She really liked Eddie and she would miss him a lot. She knew he had an ex-wife and a couple of kids up north somewhere.

"Probably, they will handle the funeral. I don't think I will go. Being a girlfriend is touchy to explain, if his ex is there," Janet told her roommate, as she climbed into her bunk.

The next morning she scanned the obituary column for more information. According to the paper Eddie was thirty-seven years old. He had told Janet that he was thirty-two. Also, the paper said that he was to be cremated. No funeral service was mentioned. Janet felt the tears coming to her eyes again.

"I wish I had spent more time with Eddie. I think I could have fallen in love with him," she told her friend.

Eddie's ex-wife received the news of his death, hours after the accident. He had left her phone number with his landlord, in case of emergency.

"Serves him right," his ex-wife had told the police. "He never did care about his family. He's two years behind in his child support and I suppose, now, you want me to pay for his funeral."

The cop didn't answer her question. Instead, he turned the whole matter over to an old, crusty insurance adjustor from Mutual Globe, who sat at his desk. He talked direct and unemotionally to this ex-wife. He had heard it all before. So, he skipped the grieving ex-widow part and went straight to the facts.

"It seems that Mr. Arroyo had one of our ten thousand dollar group-plan life insurance policies, through his previous employment at K-Mart. Since his death occurred during the thirty day grace period, even though he quit his job, his is still covered. Mrs. Arroyo, you are the beneficiary of this policy. We will be shipping the ashes of the late Mr. Arroyo to Detroit, Michigan. Once you receive them, then notify me and you will be issued a check for the remaining balance of moneys, after the cremation costs and travel expenses are paid. I will contact you, again, later in the week. My condolences, Mrs. Arroyo."

The name Mrs. Arroyo grated on her nerves. But, if it meant that she was going to get about ten thousand dollars, she could listen to it. She hated the fact that she would have to pick up his ashes and she detested the idea that the kids would have to be told. She had just met a new man, a sexy Italian and she really didn't have time for all this other stuff.

"Funny," she said, as she straightened her halter top, "Nicholas said he was from Memphis. Anyway, I'm sure he didn't know Eddie. His family owns an entertainment firm called Balushi something-or-other. Eddie's never owned a thing in his life! No, this guy is real high-class and the best thing is he likes me and the kids."

Eddie stirred on the bed. His eyes opened slightly.

"Where the hell am I," he said.

Slowly, he sat up on the edge of the bed and looked around the familiar room. Instantly, he knew he was above E.'s racketball court. Rubbing his sore forehead, he tried to remember how he had ended up in this room. All he remembered was a visit from Dr. Someti.

Washing his face in the bathroom, he smiled at his reflection. The bruising was almost gone and he looked great.

"Wonder if they got some aspirin around here," he said, as he opened the medicine cabinet. He was surprised to see his shaving equipment, deodorant and the pain pills sitting on the shelf. Grabbing a bottle of aspirin, he swallowed three pills and ran a comb through his long hair. His side burns were coming in and his black hair had just the right amount of wave. Pulling it down on his forehead, he curled up his newly sculptured lip and said, "thank-you, thank-you very much."

He didn't hear the door to his bedroom open and he didn't see the two black-suited men enter his room.

"Well asshole, you sound like him, you look like him and we are here to make sure you act like him," said the largest of the two men.

Eddie jumped, as he looked into the mirror. Reflected in its surface was a stranger's face. Pocked and swarthy-looking, this man didn't look like he was going to be Eddie's friend. Cautiously, Eddie looked around for something to defend himself with. Grabbing the can of shaving cream from the shelf, Eddie swung on the invader. In seconds Eddie was face down on the floor with a shoe on the back of his neck.

"Listen up, scum-ball. You try that again and I'll break your damn arm. Now, sit down in the chair and shut up. We got a little video to show ya," he said, pushing Eddie down hard in the chair.

Eddie sat on the chair, staring hard at the man who was blocking the door, while the other man loaded the video player with a tape.

As Eddie's two children danced across the screen, a pretty brunette in shorts and a halter top played with them.

"What the hell! That's my old lady and my kids," he yelled, as the guy in the suit pushed him back into his chair.

"They are also our insurance policy. Be a good boy, do what you're told and they stay alive."

The next scene showed a man in an intimate embrace with Eddie's ex-wife.

Somehow, this man resembled the two thugs in Eddie's room.

"Who's the slime-ball with my old lady?"

"That's our brother Nicky. He's the sweet thing's lover and our enforcer. So you see Eddie, you don't have a choice in this. Either you do it our way or the dame gets it."

Sweat broke out on Eddie's forehead. His fists were clenched so hard that the veins in his arms stood up in ugly purple lines.

"O.K., turn the T.V. off. What is it you want me to do?"

"Sorry Eddie, this was just the cartoon part of the show. The main event is coming on . . ."

The local news-caster came on the screen. Eddie watched the screen as the story of his apartment explosion unfolded. His mouth dropped open slightly when the announcer said that a Mr. Eddie Arroyo had perished in the explosion.

"What the hell," Eddie said.

The announcer finished the story with a brief interview. On the screen was his ex-boss from K-Mart. Eddie couldn't listen anymore. Rushing to the bathroom, he heaved the contents of his stomach into the toilet.

Eddie stood up at the sink and took a drink of water. Looking in the mirror, he saw the fear in his pale face. Taking a deep breath, he straightened his shoulders and walked back into the other room.

"O.K. assholes, so what do you want from me," said Eddie, as forcefully as he could.

"Just shut up and listen. This is the way it comes down, our boss is in Mexico. Depending on what the doctors think, he may be gone for sometime. You signed a contract to be the king while he is gone. Our job is to see that you fulfill this agreement. Understand?"

"Ya, all ya gotta do is be him and ya get the great treatment. Otherwise, I rearrange your face," said the other brother, doubling over with laughter.

Eddie gave the second brother an icy stare and asked about his kids.

"Ya don't have to worry about the little family, if you do what you're told."

"From what I heard, you're going to be rich, man. But, one thing, stay out of the mansion. You ain't him, understand?"

In seconds Eddie was alone. Rewinding the video tape, he listened, in disgust, as his ex-wife talked to his kids and the slimy grease-ball that has his hands all over her.

The part of the news about the fire brought tears to Eddie's eyes.

"Jesus, I'm dead, I'm friggin dead," he thought.

Eddie walked across the room and opened the door to the racketball club. The place looked deserted. Cautiously, he walked down the stairs and out onto the grounds. Everything looked so perfect. Two gardeners were mowing the lawn and the buzz of their lawn-mowers mingled with the slapping of the sprinklers. Looking behind him, he couldn't see anyone watching him. A quarter mile below him, the highway glistened in the warm sun.

"I could hitch a ride, if I got to the highway. But, then what? They'd kill my kids, my wife and me . . . that's what!" Eddie thought, as he walked back to his room in the gym.

As he lay across the bed, he thought of Janet.

"God, she thinks I'm dead. She could help me, if I told her the truth."

Reaching for the phone, Eddie picked up the receiver. The line was dead. Falling to his knee, he dropped the phone to the floor. He was trapped, trapped like a fly in a web.

An hour later, he was being escorted by the Balushi brothers to a recording studio in Collierville. Rehearsals got underway and Eddie forgot about his problems for the rest of the day. The Balushi brothers were right. Everyone thought he was E. They called him sir. They treated him like a king and by the end of the twelve days of rehearsal, Eddie thought he might just be him. One thing he was sure of was that he was having a hell of a lot of fun.

On the last day of rehearsal, Marlene showed up at the studio. She had his new costumes with her and seemed to be in high spirits.

"Well, E., you sure sound good," she said, placing the clothing bags on a chair.

"Thank ya ma'am," Eddie drawled, wondering if he should say more in the company of the studio musicians.

"You guys want to give us a little privacy," he joked, as she began unzipping his garment bags and pulling his new costumes out.

"Eddie, you look great. Are the guys treating you O.K.?"

"Ya, they're fine. But, I'm not. Marlene, these guys ain't great. They never worked with E. so they don't have a problem buying into this bull-shit. But, what about next week, when I do the Hilton in Lake Tahoe, the real back-ups will be there and I'm tellin ya, they're going to know."

"Eddie, listen to me. You've studied every move that he makes. You've learned all about his back-up singers and the band. You know the sets you're going to perform. It's only a one-night stand. Get yourself together. Jerry and I will be there with you. Now, quit worrying and try these costumes on. O.K.?" she said, hugging him.

CHAPTER FIVE

"Concert Sold Out" was the sign on the front of Hilton's box office. Eddie Arroyo was due to arrive at the Lake Tahoe Regional Airport sometime after ten o-clock and even though it was only seven in the morning, fans were already gathered in the small airport.

In Eddie's small room, three men were busy trying to get him ready, Dr. Someti, Jerry and Tony. Heaving his breakfast in the toilet, Eddie was sure he was going to die.

"Doc, ya better give him something. The plane leaves in one hour," said Tony, carrying the last of Eddie's bags down the steps to the waiting limo.

"Eddie, open the door and let me in," said Dr. Someti.

"No, I can't do this doc."

"Eddie, it's Jerry. Open the damned door and let the doc fix ya up."

Tony returned from the car and listened to their pleading.

"Hey asshole. Open the door or I'll blow the damn thing down."

Eddie slowly opened the door.

"Shit man, your face is all blotchy. What the hell is wrong with you?" said Jerry.

"Guys, this is never goin to work. I can't do it. There's goin to be thousands of people, all waiting for the real deal and shit they're goin to know. Just kill me now and get it over with," cried Eddie.

"Eddie, let me give you something to stop the vomiting and something for your nerves. You're under stress. Here take these and you will feel better."

Eddie swallowed the pills and laid down on the bed.

"Just let the medication take effect. Leave us alone for about a half an hour and Eddie will be ready to go," assured the doctor.

"I coulda got him on the plane a lot faster," said Tony, fingering his gun.

Jerry looked at Tony and rolled his eyes.

"This is goin to be a trip to remember," he thought.

Thirty minutes later, Eddie boarded the private jet and was ushered to the back bedroom. Marlene sat in the chair next to the velvet draped bed.

"Eddie, we will be landing at the Lake Tahoe airport in less than two hours. The place will be jammed with fans. So, you will be ushered out through a far terminal, at the end of the airport. The fans will catch a glimpse of you when you exit the plane. Stop at the top of the stairs and wave. Do not stop again. The boys will surround you and lead you to the limo. Do you understand?" Marlene said, concerned by the lethargic appearance of her imposter.

"Hey baby, why don't you join me for a little fun," said Eddie, as he spread out on E.'s bed. "We could really get to know each other. Have you ever screwed in the private plane," asked Eddie, blasted on pills.

"Shit, shit shit shit," said Marlene, as she stormed out into the other room in search of Someti.

Eddie dozed for the first hour of the flight. Dr. Someti joined him, as the plane prepared to land.

"Well Eddie, how are you feeling?"

"Much better, doc. I think I'm goin to make it."

Marlene entered the small room a stared at the doctor.

"Get out of here. Eddie, get up and put on these clothes."

Marlene had a black pair of tight slacks and a red satin shirt, with a high collar, in her arms. A pair of black cowboy boots and a black belt with a large silver buckle were in a travel case at the foot of the bed. Several chains, rings and a pair of silver sunglasses were also in the bag.

As Eddie stepped from the plane, no one would have known that the real man was laying in a hospital, desperately fighting for his life.

Screams and chantings and I love you greeted his ears. Eddie stopped at the top of the stairs and waved to the adoring fans. Marlene released a sigh a relief. Jerry and the boys, surrounded Eddie at the foot of the stairs, pushed Eddie to the waiting limo. In the car, Eddie stared at the screaming fans.

"Man, they really loved me," he said.

Tony started to say something. But, Jerry jabbed him hard in the ribs.

"Let the poor bastard get off on this. It'll just make my job easier," thought Jerry.

The Casino loomed, like a diamond, against the majestic blue of the Sierra-Nevada Mountains. Eddie's stomach did a little flip, as the limo pulled into the underground garage.

As he climbed from the car, he hiked up his belt and rolled up his lip. To all who saw him, he was the man, strong, sexy and famous. Employees watched from a safe distance, cooks openly greeted him and hotel management rushed to show him to his suite, as the entourage wound their way through the kitchen to the service elevator and up to the fifteenth floor.

Once inside he had minutes to gather his nerve before he was due in the theater for sound check and rehearsal.

"Jerry, is there a beer in the bar. I sure could use one," asked Eddie, as he headed for the bathroom.

"No, Jerry. No booze, he's meeting the band and back-up singers in ten minutes. Get him a Dr. Pepper, in a can," warned Marlene, thinking about the king.

Eddie noticed that his bedroom windows were covered with tin-foil and that his costumes were neatly hung in the full-wall, glass-doored closet.

"God, help me pull this off," he prayed, as he looked at his remarkable image in the mirrored door.

"Let's go," yelled Marlene.

"Got my beer," said Eddie, as he took deep strides out of the bedroom. The Dr. Pepper was thrust into his hand.

"Orders," said Jerry, casting his eyes towards an impatient Marlene.

Reporters from all forms of media coverage greeted him, as he entered the dinner-theater. Flash bulbs popped in his blue- contact covered eyes. The crew surrounded him. Pushing him forward towards the backstage entrance, Eddie let out an E. laugh and posed for a few quick pictures. One young girl had worked her way past the numerous guards and stepped out from the stage curtains, directly into him.

"I love you," she screamed.

Jerry reached in front of Eddie and lifted her body to the side of the entourage. Eddie stopped and looked at the star-struck teenager.

"Darlin, what's your name," he drawled.

"Judy," she said, reaching her hand out to touch Eddie's red sleeve. "I love you," she sighed.

Eddie bent and kissed the crying teen on the forehead. A flashbulb exploded behind him and Jerry pulled at his arm.

"E. we got to get backstage, man," he yelled, as the guards held back the approaching journalists.

Eddie looked back over his shoulder at the advancing crowd, as he slipped through the backstage door.

"God, they love me. Holy shit, what a rush," he thought, as he looked around the room at the band members and several of his back-up singers.

"I'll be right with you, man. But, right now I got a couple of things to take care of," said Eddie, as he hurried to the nearest bathroom.

Locking the door, Eddie looked at his image in the mirror. He looked like the real thing. But, he felt like Eddie.

"Shit, I'm dead. They're goin to know I'm a fake. Think about my kids . . . focus, damn it. You can do it, man," Eddie thought, as he washed his face and combed his hair.

Slowly, Eddie opened the door. Marlene was standing a few feet from the bathroom. Taking one look at Eddie's pale face, she pushed Eddie back into the bathroom and followed him inside the small cubical, locking the door.

"O.K. big boy, you can do it. You look like the man and they don't know the friggin difference. Understand?"

"Marlene, I don't know. What if I screw up?"

"Keep the conversation to a minimum, do your rehearsal and then get the hell out of the theater till show time. It'll work. It has to work, everyone is counting on us."

Those last words stung Eddie. Remembering the old, grey-haired man in the wheel chair, Eddie pulled his sagging shoulders back and unlocked the door. With a proud swagger in his walk, he marched back into the rehearsal hall.

"O.K. guys, you ready to rock?" he asked, giving them his best smile.

This was the cue to his band and the singers that the boss was in the room. Instruments were set in place. Someone handed Eddie his guitar. Bits of harmony filled the room. Eddie talked as little as possible, interject a lot of "man oh man's" in the existing chatter and laughing easily as he strummed his guitar. Then he took his mark on stage for rehearsal. His courage soared, as his magnificent voice rocked the dinner theater. The high voices of his back-up singers blended with his rich tenor, as their harmony rounded out the dynamite sound. The king was in the house and he owned the place.

His program contained some of Eddie's favorites; "Hound Dog, A Bridge Over Troubled Waters, The Wonder Of You, and ended with the Trilogy". For three hours E. and his band rehearsed without stopping. Sweat poured down Eddie's face. Stage crew members fell behind in their work, as they listened to the rehearsal. Finally, exhausted, Eddie rehearsed a short story about his mamma, his daddy and life growing up. The rehearsal was over. The final, "Thank-you, thank-you very much," was drawled out and Eddie left the stage. As the last strains of music drifted through the theater the words "E. had left the building," boomed through the P.A. system. Joyful and exhausted, the singers and band headed back to their rooms to prepare for the show. It was less than three hours till show-time, not even long enough for a nap.

Eddie followed Marlene to his suite. A huge buffet was set out in the dining area. Eddie glanced at the food and felt his stomach tighten. Walking straight to the bathroom, he threw up his Dr. Pepper.

Dr. Someti was waiting for him when he finally finished.

"Time for more meds, Eddie," said the doctor, as he prepared a shot.

"Doc, I don't know. What if I throw up on stage?"

"Just nerves, Eddie. This shot stops the muscles in your stomach from having spasms. No chance of that happening."

As the doctor injected Eddie's hip with the shot, a warm burning sensation travelled down his leg.

"Now, take these pills. They will give you energy and counteract the drowsy side effects of the shot."

Eddie's head was throbbing and he wished he was back at K-Mart. But, that life was over. After all, he was technically dead.

The pills hit immediately. His heart beat faster and he felt stronger. Pacing around his room, he felt like he was flying.

A soft knock on the door caught his attention.

Sir, my name is Arnold. It's time for me to help you get dressed for tonight's performance."

Eddie swallowed hard. Two women followed "Fast Arnold" into the room.

"Hey man, why do they call you fast?" asked Eddie.

"Sir, they think I'm slow. But, when you get out on that stage I guarantee that your jumpsuit will be properly fitted. Now, the girls are going to do your hair and make-up, if that is O.K. with you?"

Eddie drummed his fingers nervously on the bedpost and paced around the room. His mind was racing and his heart was beating so hard in his chest that it almost took his breath away.

"Man, I'm ready," he said, looking at the two ladies as they opened their make-up cases and wrapped a towel around his neck.

An hour later, Eddie looked so much like the real thing even the ladies commented on how handsome he was.

"Fast Arnold" had spent the whole hour laying out Eddie's white jumpsuit with the gold eagle emblazoned on the back. Beside it lay E.'s white shoes, cape, scarves, and huge, jeweled belt with the eagle belt buckle.

The two ladies left his bedroom and Arnold asked him if he needed to use the bathroom before final costuming.

"Man, I guess I better," laughed Eddie, as he went into the bathroom. Looking in the mirror, he admired his blue eyes with the dark mascara outline. His hair was so stiff from the hair spray that it felt artificial. His sideburns were filled in with dark eye-brow pencil and the tan make-up extended to his underwear.

"Shit, at least I'll look good when they kill me or strangle me or shoot me in the head," thought Eddie, as he felt an uncomfortable rumble in his empty stomach. "I just know I'm goin to puke on the whole first row."

"Sir, we need to move right along," said Arnold, tapping lightly on the bathroom door.

"O.K. man, lets get it over with," said Eddie, dropping his clothes to the floor.

Standing in his underwear, Eddie stepped into the heavy jumpsuit. Slowly, Arnold buttoned, snapped and zipped the costume in place. With deft hands he attached the heavy belt and showed the king how to detach the buckle, just in case "nature called." Slipping his feet into the white shoes, Eddie felt a calm come over him. He was becoming the man. The full-length glass mirrors attested to that fact. As the last ring was slipped on his finger, Marlene entered the room.

"God E., you look great," she said, motioning to Arnold to leave them alone.

"Thank you, thank you very much," Eddie laughed, feeling his confidence soaring.

Jerry opened the door. "Man, you look good," he said. "Let's go."

Eddie hiked up his belt and swept past a smiling Marlene, out into the living room of the suite. The rest of the group jumped to their feet, as he entered the room. They were all dressed in black pants, white knit shirts and black satin jackets with security printed on the back and a lightning bolt insignia on the front. Eddie looked at the insignia.

"Take care of business, that's what he would do and by God, so will I."

The ride down to the hallway leading to the theater was swift and quiet. Eddie didn't speak, therefore, no one spoke. As the doors to the back of the theater swung open that all changed. Stage hands yelled at him from all parts of the theater.

"Hey man, break a leg." "You're goin to kill them, man." "Looks like a record breakin audience."

Eddie smiled, waved and laughed. The only time his face clouded was when he looked at Tony. The little prick patted his fire-arm and smiled.

"I won't let those assholes hurt me," thought Eddie, as he gave Tony an icy stare.

Within minutes the mood backstage took on an air of extreme tension. Eddie watched the band and back-up singers, followed by his boys, take their places on stage. The house lights dimmed and the band played a few notes for warm up. Spotlights swirled across the closed curtain and the buzzing, like a thousand insects, erupted from the audience.

"Eddie, you will knock them dead," said Marlene, as she squeezed his sweating hand.

Suddenly the "Famous Entrance Theme" boomed out into the theater. His heart pounding wildly, E. stepped onto the stage for the very first time. Thunderous applause, spotlights swinging wildly from both sides of the stage, the words tumbled automatically from his mouth, as he stared blindly at the audience. He sang "Johnny Be Good" to a screaming mob of fans.

"Good evening, ladies and gentlemen. Ah, Ahhm, I'm goin to do all the songs you want to hear."

Several women shrieked and screamed as the applause grew louder. The famous sneer crossed Eddie's lips, as the guards prevented a great looking blond from climbing onto the stage from the top of the banquet table. The band started up and Eddie moved around the stage, shaking his legs and strumming his guitar, as he sang the words to "Hound Dog." Moving into "Loving You," the applause still roaring, Eddie pulled his first scarf from around his neck, wiped his dripping brow and handed it to a young brunette, who balanced herself on a chair at the front of the stage. Screams were heard, as he quickly kissed her moist lips. Hiking his belt up, he shook his long hands at his side, rolled his shoulders and laughed.

"This is too wild . . . to friggin wild," thought Eddie, as he felt the intensity of the theater lights, saw blue spots floating across his eyes from a million flash bulbs and heard the band give him the down beat on the next song.

The gospel song, "How Great Thou Art" was next. Eddie walked to the piano and took a sip of water. A hush came over the audience as he began to speak.

"My mamma and daddy took me to the First Baptist Church when I was just a little boy. This is one of my favorite gospel songs. I'd uh like to sing it for y'all."

Applause and cheers, screams and shouts and the band playing the first notes, Eddie had the audience in the palm of his hand. He could not fail. As the last song "American Trilogy" started, Eddie hated to see it end. A feeling of victory rushed through his body. As he slipped into his heavy cape, he knew what he was going to do. With all the cameras flashing and the audience roaring, Eddie, legs spread wide waited for the drum roll. Arms raised, drums pounding, crown on their feet, as the huge American Flag unrolled behind him, Eddie braced himself for the last note, a note that flew out of his throat like a comet. With the power of a super-star, he posed on one knee with his cape spread out in full glory. It was time. Reaching behind him and smiling, he unhooked his twelve hundred dollar cape and let it fly out into the audience. If the roar of the crowd hadn't been at ear-piercing level, he might have heard the unmistakable groan from Marlene. Eddie didn't care, he was the man. Taking his last posed bow, he rushed from the stage.

    He was already at the back door, when he heard the P.A. system say those famous words, "the king has left the building." Throwing himself into the backseat of the white limo, he wrapped a towel around his neck and closed his eyes. The roar of the crowd still thundered in his ears and his heart felt like it was about to crash out of his chest.

Dr. Someti, Marlene, Tony and two of his boys jammed in the car after Eddie.

"Man, you were great," said one of the group.

"Because of your performance, E. will live," said Dr. Someti.

Eddie removed the towel from his face and looked at the doctor. A spasm wracked his body. Vomiting into the towel, he wiped his mouth and laid his head back on the seat.

"Hey man, throw that towel out the window. Bet some chick wants it for a souvenir," laughed Tony, opening the tinted window and tossing the terry towel out onto the highway.

"Hey you guys, shut the hell up and let the man sleep," said Marlene, looking at a very exhausted Eddie.

CHAPTER SIX

Eddie slept for an hour. When he awoke the limo had left Lake Tahoe and was entering Placer County. Making a right hand turn at the Placerville exit, Eddie opened his eyes and looked out the car window. Houses, their windows dark, appeared through the thick pine trees. At the end of a blind street, called Ellie's Alley, the car climbed a steep driveway leading up to a two-story house. Eddie heard the whir of the garage door opener, as the large limo disappeared into the garage.

"Well, they're goin to kill me now. Shit, that's why they drove out to this friggin house," thought Eddie, allowing his paranoia to cloud his mind.

Eddie heard Jerry say, "Hey man, get out." Marlene and the doctor were already unloading suitcases from the trunk. Eddie, shook his head, trying to clear his mind.

"Eddie, you O.K.?" asked Marlene, as she stuck her head into the car.

"Uh, yah, I'm fine," replied Eddie, as he started to get out of the car.

Tony looked at Marlene and signaled for her to go on in the house. He stepped into the shadows of the garage and waited for Eddie to try something.

"Come on asshole, make a run for it or something. I'll plug ya before ya f-in get six feet," thought Tony, fingering his gun.

Eddie stared up at the star filled sky. The stars seemed close enough to touch with his hands. He could hear the sounds of voices in the house and wondered if he could just walk down the drive-way and disappear into the night. Then he looked down at the rhinestone-covered jump-suit and laughed. Turning towards the house, he climbed the stairs and opened the kitchen door.

"Hey Eddie, your clothes are in the upstairs bedroom. You pulled it off, man," said Jerry, as he walked past him into the living-room.

The kitchen door slammed, as Tony came into the house. The T.V. blared in the living room. Everyone acted like they were at home.

Eddie climbed the stairs to his room. His legs were tired and he had a head-ache. Marlene sat in his room, filing her nails.

"Where are we," asked Eddie.

"A friend's house," replied Marlene, opening Eddie's suitcase. "Get a shower, then come on downstairs for some breakfast."

Eddie walked into the bathroom, removed his white jump-suit, the jewelry, his glasses, stepped out of his white shoes and kicked his shorts off with his foot. The shower was strong and the hot water felt great. Tan puddles gathered at his feet. His make-up slid from his tired body. As he toweled off, he rubbed his burning stomach. Wiping the mirror with the end of his towel, he stared at his image. What he saw startled him. His eyes were blood red, from the sweat and contacts, his hair was jet-black and wild-looking and his pale skin gave him a ghostly, maniacal appearance.

"What's happening to me?" he thought, as he eased the blue contacts onto his finger.

He knew that he was getting an ulcer.

"Soon Someti will be treatin me for this . . . that is if I live that long. They're probably lyin about everything. E. in Mexico, that's probably another lie. Marlene's a lyin bitch. God, my stomach is killin me," thought Eddie.

In his suitcase he found the bottle of anti-nausea medicine. Swallowing two pills, he slipped his black pants and shirt onto his damp body. His Rockports were on the floor. As he pushed his bare feet into them, he could smell the tantalizing smell of bacon cooking. Running a comb quickly through his hair, he ran down the steps to the kitchen.

"Want some breakfast?" asked Jerry, as he handed Eddie a cup of coffee.

Eddie sat down at the table, while Marlene placed a plate full of eggs, bacon, muffins and grits in front of Eddie.

"Thanks, I guess I'm hungry."

"Look at the paper. Damn, you got great reviews," said Marlene.

Eddie took another large mouthful of eggs and reached for the morning paper. A picture of him, his arm outstretched to an adoring fan, graced the entertainments section. The caption read, "Star wows fans at sold out concert". Eddie read the article, feeling a cold shiver run up his spine, as the reality of his actions hit him.

"They bought it. Eddie Arroyo is dead and the fans think I'm the man. But, I'm not . . . I'm, I'm. Who am I?" Eddie asked.

Dr. Someti looked at Eddie and got up from the breakfast table. Standing next to Marlene at the stove, he whispered in her ear.

"Better get his mind off this, or where going to have trouble on our hands."

Eddie wiped his eyes and took another bite of his breakfast. All he wanted to do was get away from these people and get his little life back. Suspiciously, he looked at the doctor.

"How come you're not eating any breakfast, doc?" he asked, as he looked at his plate, noticing that everyone else was eating doughnuts.

"Already ate, Eddie," said the doctor, showing some nervousness in his voice.

Marlene walked over to the table and sat down next to Eddie. Reaching into her purse, she pulled out a white envelope.

"Hey Eddie, smile, everything is cool. Heard from E. this morning. He thought you were great. Oh, here's the $28,000 for the show and your training. Not bad, Eddie . . . Not bad for a two hour show.

Reaching for the envelope, Eddie pushed his chair back and stood up from the table.

"Man, I got my money, I did my job, I want to go out and spend it."

Jerry rose from his chair, a habit stemming from his years with his boss. He was ready to go help this man spend his money, too.

"Everyone, relax. We will be heading back to Memphis soon, then we're all going shopping. Just relax, no concerts for two weeks, Eddie. Plenty of time for fun," said Marlene.

Eddie didn't want to relax. As he turned on his heel and headed up the stairs, his mind was working overtime.

"If I go out the bedroom window, I'll break my neck. If I try to escape, they'll shoot me or my family. I'm screwed," thought Eddie, as he lay across the bed, suddenly feeling very sleepy.

Dr. Someti pulled up Eddie's eyelid, took his blood-pressure and drew a small vial of blood from Eddie's vein.

"I'll be right back," Someti said to Marlene. "Keep an eye on him. His breathing is a little irregular."

In the basement, Dr. Someti set up his portable lab and did some tests. Not pleased with the results, he returned to Eddie's room.

"Blood's not bad, but his respiration is too fast. Let's slow this down," he said, as he injected Eddie with a shot.

"Doc, you better get this right. He's got to last till everything is in place," said Marlene.

"I think I've got it, now. Just let him sleep."

Eddie awoke at dusk, sweating profusely. Grabbing the dresser to steady himself, he fell to his knees in front of the toilet. Once again, he emptied the contents of his stomach.

"Damn, what the hell is wrong with me?" cried Eddie, wiping his mouth with the towel.

Eddie listened for noise from the lower rooms. Everything seemed quiet. Grabbing his envelope of money from the bed, he slipped down the stairs and out the back door.

"Goin somewhere," said Tony, as Eddie looked behind him, into the barrel of a gun.

Eddie, his heart beating wildly, felt the earth flip up to meet him, as he leaned against the steps.

"Jesus Tony, what the hell ya doin," yelled Dr. Someti, as he rushed to help Eddie to his feet.

"Eddie, are you O.K.? You look like you are going to pass out."

"It's my heart, doc. It feels strange."

"Eddie, listen to me. Do you have any numbness in your arms? Is there pain in your chest?"

"No, no pain. It feels like it's beatin itself to death. Listen. Can't ya hear it?"

"Breathe deeply. Let's walk together a little. Can you do that?" said Someti as he walked across the crest at the steep driveway.

Slowly, Eddie's respiration slowed. The sun was setting and the air was cooler. Eddie looked at the brush covered hillside and knew that there was no escaping this prison.

Sitting on a tree stump, Eddie looked at the doctor.

"Are you guys goin to kill me?"

"I'm sorry Tony scared you. We don't want to harm you. Eddie, have you ever heard of the "Witness Protection Program"? Well Eddie, you might consider your job like being in the program. Right now, you are very valuable. For all intentions and purposes, you are him. When E. comes back, you can disappear; tint your hair, lose weight, grow a beard . . . You'll be all right. Murder is not a part of this, I assure you. You can travel wherever you want on new fake I.D.'s and you'll have the money to do it."

Eddie closed his eyes and thought of his family, his girl, his simple life. When he opened his eyes, the doctor had walked back to the house. Eddie, feeling better, stood up and walked down the driveway. Jumping to the side of the drive, he watched as a blue Mercedes roared up the steep driveway, screeching to a halt.

"Damn, didn't see you," yelled Marlene, as she opened the door and stepped out of the little car.

"Jesus, Marlene, ya almost mowed me down."

Grinding her cigarette out under her black heel, she walked over to Eddie and put her arms around his neck.

"Speed gets me excited. I guess I was thinking about my big stud when I should have been watching my driving. Marlene will make it up to you," she said, licking his earlobe.

Eddie raised his arms, pushing her away.

"You bitch, you're a part of this. You trapped me. You're probably behind the whole thing to kill my family," said Eddie, feeling his heart, once again, racing in his chest.

Not missing a beat, Marlene looked at Eddie, tears glistening in her pretty eyes.

"Eddie, it's not like that. I'm trapped the same way you are. They are forcing me to stay here, just like you. Eddie, I'm scared," she cried.

"What do you mean, they got you?"

"Shhhsh Eddie, they'll hear us. Let's go upstairs and I'll tell you the truth," said Marlene, taking Eddie's clammy hand in hers and leading him into the house and up the stairs to his bedroom.

Jerry stared at Marlene, as she clung to Eddie. Going to the door, he looked out at the Mercedes, its dome light shining from the open door. Marlene's briefcase lay in the center of the walkway, where she had dropped it. Shaking his head, he walked down to the car and closed the door. Tony, followed out to the driveway.

"What's up, Jerry?"

"Christ, I don't know. Looks like he is really doin the E. thing with Marlene."

"Too bad he's doin it with a man," laughed Tony.

As the door closed to Eddie's bedroom, Marlene let the tears flow.

"Eddie, I didn't know anything. These are some bad people. Please baby, let's help each other."

"Why should I believe anything you say?"

Marlene reached her hand out, pulled Eddie's belt tighter, then released the clasp, his Levis slid over his hips and bunched around his ankles. In his confusion and fear, he found himself becoming aroused. Pushing Marlene back on the bed, Eddie climbed on top of her. In seconds Marlene was staring at the ceiling of Eddie's bedroom, teeth clenched, thinking of Audrey.

"Oh God, this is disgusting . . . just finish and get the hell off of me," thought Marlene, moaning.

In minutes, it was over. Marlene lit her cigarette, inhaling deeply. Eddie reached his arm out to encircle her, but Marlene was already sliding from the bed.

"Come back here, darling," he moaned, as he watched her slip into his terry robe.

"Eddie I want to, but I have to go downstairs. I have something to show you. I'll be right back. You just keep that sexy motor runnin," she said, as she slipped from the bedroom.

On the landing of the stairs, Marlene was stopped by Tony.

"So, how was it with a man, Marlene?"

Jerry, laughed as Marlene gave Tony a hard kneeing in the crotch.

"So, did you do it with him?" Jerry yelled.

"Wise-ass, you do it with him, if you think it's so fun," she said as she ground her cigarette into Jerry's plate of food.

Jerry's face reddened, as foul words and curses tumbled from his mouth. Doctor Someti was still laughing, as Marlene picked up her briefcase from the kitchen table and disappeared up the stairs.

Eddie, his eyes half closed, threw back the covers, as Marlene entered the room.

"Come on back to bed, woman."

"Eddie, look," she said, as she opened her briefcase, taking a large manilla envelope from the inside compartment.

Eddie stared at the two airline tickets to Mexico, car keys and phone numbers.

"This is our escape package," she said, smiling.

"Mexico, you and I?"

"Yes. When E. comes back, we get the hell outa here. You'll have all the money. We could be so happy. You're such a stud."

"Things are gettin better," thought Eddie, as he sat naked on the bed, planning a trip to Mexico, with Marlene.

CHAPTER SEVEN

Eddie's fears lessened, as he thought about a new life, a life with money and Marlene. Returning to the mansion was a thrill. The grounds look palatial to Eddie, as the limo pulled up in front of the white lions that flanked the entrance to the house.

"I feel like E. with my girl," thought Eddie, as he and Marlene walked through the front door.

"Eddie, you wait here," said Marlene, as she entered the closed doors leading to the dining room.

Sitting on the steps leading up to the bedrooms, Eddie stared at the picture of the king that hung at the top of the stairs.

"His home, man-oh-man, I'm in the man's home."

Eddie's daydream was interrupted by Marlene.

"Your employer wants a word with you," she said, as she stuck her head out of the doors that enclosed the dining room.

In an arm-chair, at the end of the long dining table, sat a man with short, white hair. He appeared heavy, dressed in a jogging suit with a baseball cap and dark glasses on his head. As

Eddie approached the man, he noticed that he wasn't sitting in an arm-chair. He was sitting in a heavily padded wheelchair. A nurse, dressed in a starched white uniform, stood behind the man.

"Hey, this can't be the king. Not this sick old man," thought Eddie, as he looked closely at the face of the wheelchair bound man.

"Come on in, man. Join the party. Great job in Tahoe, ya made me proud. Are my boys takin care of ya?" he said, as he laid his head back on the padded wheelchair.

"Ah, ya. Everything's fine, sir. Thanks," Eddie stuttered, trying not to stare at his boss.

A harsh coughing spell doubled the great one over, as the nurse sprayed a medication into his mouth. Eddie felt his fingernails dig into the palms of his hands, as he tensed.

"I, I'm goin away for treatment. Ya see, I'm off all my meds. It's hard . . . I just want to thank ya, man," E. whispered.

Eddie walked over to the wheelchair. Falling down on his knees, he looked into the mirrored glasses and barely recognizable face of his idol. With tenderness, he touched the legend's hand.

"Get well, man. I love ya. The whole world loves ya." As he started to answer Eddie, another coughing fit ripped through his body, Fearing that he was upsetting him, Eddie stood up and backed away. The nurse rolled her patient into the adjoining kitchen. Jerry followed her, pulling the I.V. bags that connected to his boss, behind the wheelchair.

"My God," choked Eddie. "He looks bad."

Marlene wiped the tears from her eyes and nodded her head at Eddie.

"I gotta get some air," Eddie replied, wiping the tears from his eyes with the back of his big hand.

Eddie walked out the side door of the mansion, past the swimming pool and up the hill to the racket-ball club. As the side door closed, muffled laughter rang through the kitchen . . .

Marlene, her foot on a kitchen chair, leaned over to Jerry and lit her cigarette.

"I don't know how much more of this crap I can stand."

"Lighten up Marlene," said Jerry. "Everything went well. The performance went off without a hitch. He's got his fifty bucks. Not bad, for ten minutes of acting and Someti's taking him home on the train."

"Ya, so far everything's O.K., but what if someone talks?"

"Someti's got the kid covered. So, just stop worrying."

As the train approached Rockford, Illinois, a young man suffered a fatal heart attack. A doctor from Memphis tried to revive the young man, but he was pronounced dead at Rockford Memorial Hospital. He was a drama student from Rock Valley College. His girlfriend said he was auditioning for a play in Memphis. His case contained make-up, wigs and his driver's license. She had no knowledge that he had a bad heart.

His funeral is scheduled for tomorrow. He is an orphan, with no known family.

"See Marlene," said Jerry, as he read the article from the Rockford Register Republic. "All the bases are covered."

Marlene turned over on her back. The sun felt good and she enjoyed swimming in the pool.

"Have you checked on Eddie? He's got rehearsal tonight and I haven't seen him since this morning."

"Ya, Marlene. He's fine. Tony's keepin an eye on him and Someti's due back tonight. Have you heard from E.?"

Marlene sat up in her deck chair at the mention of her boss.

"Well, this is strictly on the Q.T., but I heard that he is in Isreal."

"According to guys, they got word of a donor in Israel. He left Mexico early yesterday and they landed in Israel sometime during the early hours this morning. That's all I know."

Eddie took the calendar from the wall and marked off one more day. Ten days and he would be back on stage. His face was healed and the bluish marks around his nose were gone.

"You can fool some of the people some of the time," thought Eddie, as he curled his lip and looked at his remarkable face.

"My gosh, if the public could see the real king, no one would recognize him! What the hell am I worried about," thought Eddie, feeling cocky about his looks and sad about his boss.

"I wish I could talk to him. He could give me some idea about what I need to do," thought Eddie, as he walked out of his bedroom and onto the grounds.

As he approached the pool, he saw Marlene. She had unsnapped the top of her two-piece suite and was lying on her stomach. Quietly, he opened the gate and walked over to her chaise lounge.

"Need some suntan lotion," he whispered in her ear.

"What," she replied, sitting up in the chair.

"My God, Baby, you got great tits," Eddie said.

Marlene looked at Eddie's face, that remarkable chiseled nose, those deep blue eyes and that long black hair. Even in the bright sunlight, he looked like him. Turning to face Eddie she made no move to cover her breasts.

"I thought you promised some suntan lotion."

Eddie reached for the bottle of oil from beside the chair, but Marlene was too fast. Diving into the pool, she swam to the deep end. Eddie stood up and looked at his clothes. The silk shirt, black cowboy boots and black pants were not going to get him to Marlene. Laughing, he walked over to the edge of the pool.

"You are as slippery as a snake, but I'm patient. Why don't ya get out of that pool and let ol stud-man dry ya off."

"Sorry Eddie, I've got to get to my exercise. Maybe, later," said Marlene, as she dove to the bottom of the pool.

Smiling to himself, Eddie left the pool and walked back to the house. He had two hours before rehearsal and if he couldn't screw Marlene, he'd eat the lunch that he left sitting in his room.

An hour later, he was in the limo with Jerry, on his way to rehearsal. The studio musicians worked hard and Eddie's voice seemed to be in good shape. This next concert was to last for three nights, in Vegas. So, Eddie needed more time to learn the new songs and polish his performance. It was almost two in the morning before they called it a rap. Jerry was asleep in the outer recording office.

"Hey man, let's go," said Eddie, as he nudged Jerry.

"I'm goin to stay. The little blond back-up singer and I are goin to party for a while," said Jerry.

Eddie looked at the blond and smiled. She looked to be about sixteen in the face, but her tight sweater and black leotard made her seem much older. As Eddie walked out the door, she was climbing onto the couch with Jerry.

The limo driver was waiting outside and as Eddie climbed into the back seat of the car, he wondered if Marlene would be waiting for him

The mansion looked deserted, as the limo driver dropped him at the front door. All the lights were off and the parking spaces behind the house were empty. In the racketball club, he switched on a light and climbed the stairs to his room. Marlene was not waiting for him.

"Damn," he said, as he looked around the empty room. "Maybe the cook's still up," he said, feeling a need to fill his empty stomach.

Eddie was not allowed to go to the main house. These rules were explicit and as he walked across the grass to the back door, he looked into the shadows for Tony or some other monster to jump out at him or shoot him. The place was deserted. Slowly, he tried the back door and to his surprise, it opened.

"I'll just get myself a sandwich and a coke," he said, as he walked into the kitchen. The light above the stove was on. Within minutes, he had a huge ham sandwich, potato salad, pickles and a soft drink. As he crossed the kitchen towards the back door, he saw the telephone.

Carefully, he picked up the cradle and listened to the dial tone. From memory, he dialed his girl at the army base in Millington. After three rings, a sleepy voice answered the phone.

"Hello."

"Baby, it's me Eddie. I've missed you," he said, feeling relieved to talk to her.

"Who the hell is this? You pervert!"

"Baby, it's me. Don't hang up," begged Eddie.

"Grave-robbin bastard, don't call here again," she yelled, slamming the phone in Eddie's ear.

Eddie stared at the phone, placed the call again and listened to it ring fifteen times, while a tear slid from his eye.

"Damn them, she thinks I'm dead. Everyone thinks I'm dead. What would I tell the police? Shit, Eddie Arroyo is dead. I'm not him. I've been kidnapped and forced to be E. That'll make the cops rush right over here and save me. Oh ya, and by the way, I'm standing in the kitchen of his mansion, eating a ham sandwich. You'll know who I am, I'm the one in the black silk shirt with the sideburns. I'm screwed, that's the truth," thought Eddie, crying at the absurdity of his situation.

Hanging up the phone, Eddie picked up a bottle of scotch from the kitchen counter and headed out the back door to his bedroom.

Lying on the bed, in his shorts, Eddie drank a third of the bottle.

"Well, maybe E. will get back after this concert and then I can start a new life in Mexico with Marlene. The booze had calmed his nerves and he was getting sleepy. It was almost daylight out. As he closed his eyes, he heard the crunch of tires driving up the gravel drive.

"Jerry's girl is driving him home, or Tony is getting in or Marlene is coming to sleep with me, who give's a shit," thought Eddie, as he slipped into a drunken sleep.

CHAPTER EIGHT

To a man who had never been out of the country, except for his tour in Germany, landing in Israel was a strange experience for him. The airport was busy, filled to capacity with tourists, students and the strangest sight he had ever seen, Orthodox Jews. Their long black coats, high black hats, massive beards and long, curly sideburns fascinated him.

"Man-oh-man, and all my life they said I dressed strange," as he stared at a child and his father, both Orthodox Jews.

"The little uns look just like their daddy, only smaller, kinda spooky."

Bart Joseph Anderson, his male nurse, smiled at this comment, Bart pushed E.'s wheelchair to the V.I.P. lounge. He had been with him for almost two months, after being hired as a private-duty nurse during his last stay at Baptist Memorial. According to E., he was as good as any of the doctors that worked on him and a lot more entertaining to be around.

Chris and Don, two of E.'s closest friends also accompanied him on this trip. They had never been out of the South and appeared confused by the different languages they heard.

"Hey man, I think we should have stayed in Mexico. It's dangerous to be in a country full of Jews and they are all carrying guns," said Chris.

"Relax. Just get the limo driver to pull around to the V.I.P. exit and we'll be outta here. Nix the kike jokes, though," laughed Don.

E. tried to laugh at their humor, but he had been off his medication for almost twenty-four hours and he was having trouble breathing.

"Bart Joseph, can ya get me anything for the pain," he asked between coughing attacks.

Bart Joseph looked at his boss, his arms and legs weak and shaky, his face golden and bloated and knew that he was terminal. If this liver transplant failed, he would not return to Memphis. Reaching into his bag, he took out a hypodermic needle and filled it with the proper amount of Morphine. As he rolled up E.'s sleeve, he distracted him by asking a question that had haunted him for the last two months.

"Sir, how did you get this crescent scar on your bicep?"

He looked at Bart Joseph and smiled. Coughing, he told the story.

"Well man, Mary was in the kitchen getting ready to fry up a mess of banana sandwiches for me and the boys. Marty was throwing a soccer ball at me and I thought I had it. The ball hit the pan, the pan hit my arm and the grease hit everything. I laughed so hard when I saw Mary chasin Marty across the kitchen with the pan, that I didn't know I was burnt. By the time it started stinging, the scar was already set, blistering and poppin, so that's where I got the crescent moon on my arm. Thanks for the shot, man, I can feel it in my lips."

The hospital was located on top of Mt. Carmel. He was in less pain by the time he arrived and slipped into a deep sleep as soon as the nurses got him to his private suite. Bart Joseph stayed right by him, having a sleeping bed set up next to his bed. The hardest thing for Bart Joseph was remembering to call his boss by his new alias, Jesse Sanders. The story was that Jesse was an executive with the General Motors Corporation. Looking at his boss, he thought the story would probably work. E.'s hair was white, as was his short beard. His face had a sickly yellow tinge and his blue eyes were barely visible beneath his swollen eyelids and puffed face. He wore a gold cross and a bronze Star of David around his neck and his body was swollen and trembling. He didn't resemble the king, except for the crescent scar on his arm.

A team of doctors were ready for Mr. Sanders. The liver that was to be transplanted belonged to a young man who had suffered a fatal auto accident two days ago. Thanks to his donor card, he was being preserved on life support, until the team could get their patient to the hospital. The surgery was scheduled for late this afternoon. As E. slept, tests were being conducted. This was a very risky surgery, and all the necessary precautions were being taken to assure its success. Mr. Sanders knew the risks and the odds of its success.

"Man, I might as well be dead. I can't sing, shit I can't even walk. Someti says it might give me a year." He sounded sad as he talked to Ginny, his girlfriend.

"Look, I think you should go for it. I love you and I don't want to lose you. I'll stay here in

Mexico for a couple days, like we planned. When the surgery is over and the coast is clear, I'll be right by your side in Israel. Be brave, my darling," said Ginny, tears running down her cheeks, as she kissed her love good-bye, when he left for Israel.

E. could hear the voices of the two interns as they discussed his chart. Bart Joseph was out of the room and he appeared to be sound asleep.

"High blood pressure, distinct heart murmur, poor physical condition, a severe addiction to prescription drugs, why is Dr. Chaim ben ha Kohn risking his reputation on such a poor candidate?"

"Don't know. Must be someone pretty important, a national treasure in America or something," answered the other orderly.

"Here comes the male nurse. You want to tell him, or should I?"

"You do it."

Bart Joseph entered the room, eating a candy bar. He looked at the two orderlies and smiled, "Everything O.K. with my boss?" E. still pretended to sleep.

"Mr. Anderson, we have received orders that you must vacate Mr. Sanders' room. Dr. Kohn feels that you have no medical authority here in Israel and would appreciate your cooperation in this matter. A full-time nurse of Dr. Kohn's, will replace you. Is this going to be a problem?"

Bart Joseph stared at the orderly, his mouth slightly open.

"What the hell. I don't friggin work for you guys, I work for E., I mean Sanders," said Bart Joseph, his voice becoming high and shrill.

Two security guards appeared at the door. Bart looked at the two beefy Israeli's and picked up his suitcase. Quietly, he left the room and the hospital.

"Did you hear what I heard? Star Power, you don't think that fag meant the king do you?" said one of the orderlies, as they walked down the hall.

"Eric, did that fat man look like him to you? No, I didn't think so. Anyway, how can you believe anything from a man whose medical procedures included enemas, water pills and all the demoral he could stuff down that poor man. It's a wonder his liver lasted long enough for a transplant."

By lunch, Eric and his girlfriend, Nurse Gerda Krypka, had changed their mind about the mystery patient. Gerda had been assigned to handle the admittance and something didn't figure.

"Eric, Mr. Sanders' address is listed as Tennessee. Don't you think that's a little too coincidental?"

"Also, Margot says that this guy has a cross and a Star of David on his necklace. I have a picture of him in my movie magazine, and he's wearing a gold cross and a bronze Star of David. I think it's him."

Dr. Kohn wasn't concerned about music. He was concerned about the condition of his patient. As he sat in Mr. Sanders' room, watching the labored breathing of his patient, he wondered if the transplant would save this man's life. One fact he was sure of, with the liver damage this man had sustained, he would die without the transplant. E. opened his eyes and smiled at the doctor.

"Mr. Sanders, I'm Dr. Kohn. We talked on the phone. I would like to go over your surgery with you, if you are alert."

He rolled over on his side and looked at the doctor.

"Doc, I feel like I'm in the valley of the shadow of death? Do you think you can help me?"

"Mr. Sanders, I'm not going to lie to you. This surgery is very risky and I'm inclined to leave your survival to the Lord."

"That's what I'm talking about, doc. I would like to make my peace with the Lord. Can you help me?"

Dr. Kohn, a survivor of the death camps leaned forward and whispered in his patient's ear, "I have seen people on the side of death, with the grim reaper's grip firmly attached. Then, Death loses his grip and the sun's rays come back into their being. It could be so with you. Pray to your God."

For the next hour he listened to the risks of brain damage, death from cardiac arrest and possible organ rejection. Finally, the doctor laid the release forms on his night table and asked him to read them over and sign them. Without a shred of fear, he picked up the pen and signed the forms, using his real name. The doctor looked at the famous signature and sighed. These papers would not be put in his file for several weeks. Dr. Kohn had already heard rumors of newspaper men trying to get to his famous patient, disguised as Rabbis, telegram delivery men and orderlies. He'd put up with the guards, but a room full of screaming fans wouldn't be healthy for his patient.

As Mr. Sanders was wheeled to the operating room, the doctor said a short prayer, the same prayer he would have performed for a pauper or the man. The surgery would last approximately twelve hours and his team was waiting for him in the operating theater. Concern clouded the doctor's face, as he checked his patient's vital signs. His heart rate was erratic and his breathing was labored. Maccabee Hospital was famous for experimental surgery and this surgery was one of the riskiest.

The reality of his surgery, the cold sterile room, trays of strange instruments and doctors cloaked in white gowns caused him to shake. As the doctor turned him face down on the operating table, he told the doctor that he was in the Lord's hands. Then, looking around the room, he admired how clean everything was. An I.V. was inserted in his left arm, and an injection was administered. First, he felt a wave of nausea engulf him. Breathing deeply, he drifted. His mother's face appeared before him. She was feeding chickens outside the back door of the mansion. He saw her run to him, calling his name, then darkness.

"Mr. Sanders is ready, doctor," said the anesthesiologist.

The large incision was made in his back, revealing an enlarged, hard, black liver, connected to severely clogged arteries. It was twice its normal size. A few minutes later the team had extracted the dysfunctional organ. For the next ten hours the team worked to connect the transplanted liver to their patient. The patient slipped into a deep coma, unaware of his body. Pulsating machines monitored his vitals and as the deep incision was finally closed, the O.R. was deathly silent. Mr. Sanders had survived the surgery. But, as he was placed on a ventilator and reconnected to monitors in the intensive care unit, the doctor wondered if his patient would ever regain consciousness.

The liver team wondered the same thing.

"I don't know," said one of the doctors, "if he had only come to Dr. Kohn sooner. You know, sometimes the operation is a success and the patient dies. Let's hope the man has a great will to live."

Dr. Kohn agreed with his team, as he changed out of his blood-splattered scrubs. He still had to meet with the relatives and friends of his patient.

"Mr. Sanders survived the procedure. Now, the next twenty-four hours will tell us if his body will accept or reject the new liver," he told Chris and Don.

CHAPTER NINE

By morning, news had reached the streets that rumors of an American legend had been admitted to Maccabee Hospital with a life-threatening illness. By noon, the gossip mongers had reported that he had, indeed, come to Israel to die. People drove and walked to the hospital.

Gathering in the parking lot, they gazed up at the six windows on the tenth floor. It was reported that this was the room the legend was staying in and the tin-foil covered glass did little to dispel their beliefs. An Orthodox Jew, his long beard swaying in the breeze, rocked back and forth on his heels. Fans scorned him, as he performed the mourner's Kiddish, a prayer for the dead. Their idol was not going to die.

By evening, the news broke world-wide. A reporter for the *Haifa Gossip Gazette* reported this story, "It has been reported to me that a man wearing a cross and a Star of David, a man from Tennessee, has been admitted to Maccabee Hospital. People gathering outside the hospital say that the whole tenth floor of the hospital has been sealed off to the public. Six windows are sealed with what appears to be tinfoil and guards are posted at the entrance to the floor. If this is, indeed, the famous king, than the question is, who will be performing this weekend in Las

Vegas, Nevada? We will keep you abreast of this mystery, as it unfolds."

Marlene received the call at her home office phone. Stunned to hear of the allegations that had already spread through the hospital in Israel, she immediately denied the rumor.

"No comment, my boss is well and looking forward to entertaining his fans this weekend in Las Vegas. No, he has never been to Israel and has no knowledge of a life-threatening illness."

Marlene, her hands shaking, called Jerry at the mansion.

"What the hell is goin on? I just received a call from a rag in Israel. Somehow, they got wind that E. is in the hospital. Get on the phone to the boys and find out what is goin on. Handle this Jerry, or by God I'll have your hide. You're in charge of P.R., damn it."

By afternoon the phone was ringing off the hook. The *Memphis Gazette* was threatening to run the story on the front page and wanted a personal interview with their idol. Fans gathered at the gate, hoping to catch a glimpse of him and ticket sales soared. Jerry called Haifa and confirmed that his boss was still in intensive care. According to the guys, no one, except the male nurse, could have leaked the story. According to Chris, the doctor had insisted on replacing Bart Joseph and he had left yesterday on a flight home.

"Marlene, I think it was the nurse that leaked the story." He's back in town and Someti is goin to pay him a little visit. I think we better get Eddie ready for his first interview. The guys from the *Gazette* are coming to the mansion this afternoon and the fans really need to see Eddie on the grounds. Hope the asshole can carry this off," yelled Jerry.

"Jerry, let me talk to Eddie. He's not aware of this problem, yet. I can get him to do it for me."

Eddie was in the shower when Marlene opened his bedroom door and walked into the bathroom.

"Eddie, it's Marlene. You want to come out here, or would you like some company," she said, pulling open the plastic shower curtain.

"Hey baby, you know what Eddie likes," he said, turning his soapy body to her and reaching out his arms.

Marlene dropped her clothes to the floor and climbed into the shower. As Eddie rubbed her breasts, she told him about the surgery in Israel. A sadness overcame his passion, as he thought of his idol lying in intensive care in some foreign country.

"Baby, I wish there was somethin I could do to help him get well."

Jumping at the opportunity, Marlene wasted no time telling Eddie about the rumors and reporters.

"Geez, you mean you want me to talk to those guys. They've interview the real deal and you want me to fool them?"

"Eddie, baby, I know you can do it. You fool me all the time," she said, as she ran her fingers down his naked, wet chest.

"O.K., if you think so. I'll do it. Just tell me what you want and your stud will do it."

Marlene stepped from the shower and toweled herself dry. Eddie looked disappointed, as she slipped her skirt and blouse on and walked into the bedroom. By the door were a cassette recorder and a mike.

"I've written down what you are to say. Read it over and practice saying it into the tape player. I'll be back in an hour and we will see if you've got it. O.K.?"

"Ya, I guess. But, do ya have to go, baby?"

Marlene was already out the door and heading back to her office. Her hair was wet and she needed some make-up. Also, she had smoked her last cigarette in the pack and was thinking of killing someone if she didn't get another pack soon.

"Tammy, get me some cigarettes, a hair dryer and a cup of coffee," she barked as she entered the office.

Tammy looked at her boss. Her hair was wet and the front of her blouse had damp spots on its silk fabric. She knew that Marlene had been to the mansion for the last hour. Now, as she opened her purse and took out a fresh pack of cigarettes for Marlene, she wondered how come her boss looked like she had just stepped out of the shower.

"Here's your smokes, Marlene. But, where can I find a hair dryer? You look like you just got out of a shower."

Marlene lit a cigarette and looked at Tammy. She was such a dummy, but, maybe she could use this to her benefit.

"Tammy, can you keep a secret?"

"Sure Marlene. My lips are sealed," replied Tammy, as she pulled up a chair close to Marlene's desk.

"Well, you know the rumors that are flyin around about our boss?"

"You mean that he's in Israel and sick. I can't believe those news people. If he was sick, we'd know it, wouldn't we?"

"Of course we could. He's just fine. In fact, when I went over to the mansion to ask him about the interview he has tonight with the *Memphis Gazette*, he was feeling so good that we had a little play time in the shower, if you know what I mean."

Tammy's mouth dropped open as she thought about her two bosses making love in the shower of the mansion. She could hardly wait to call her friend and tell her the news. Tonight she would be a real hit at the fan-club meeting. She had some inside dirt on her bosses and the girls were just going to die when they hear the details.

"I think I can get your hair up in a twist, if you like," offered Tammy.

"Thanks, but it's almost dry. You can go now. Thanks for the cigarettes," said Marlene, smiling smugly.

Eddie practiced his speech and his movements in front of the mirror. By seven o'clock he was dressed in a purple suit, gold silk shirt and silver jewelry. As he swaggered around the bedroom he felt like the man.

"Eddie, it's Marlene," she said, as she opened the door to his room.

"Geez, you look great. That's even his suit. Jerry bring it over?"

Eddie looked down at his suit and ran his large hand over the shiny fabric.

"My God, I'm wearin the king's clothes," he thought, curling up his lip and saying, "thank-you, thank-you very much."

"Let's get over to the mansion. The reporters will be here in less than an hour and we are going to have the interview in the downstairs living room.

At eight a camera crew set up their lights and mikes in the hallway adjoining the colorful room. Eddie sat in a high-backed red velvet chair. His jet-black hair and bright purple suit made him look healthy and regal. To all the camera men he looked like the king. Wayne Morris of channel five conducted the interview and he was visibly nervous.

Sir, I do apologize for this inconvenience. I mean, all you have to do is look at you and you can see that you look great."

"Hey man, don't sweat it. My fans need to know that I'm fine and this is the best way for me to stop this foolishness. So, if you're ready, let's do it."

The ten minute news special started with a collage of photos of Eddie's last performance in Tahoe. Then the words of Wayne Morris, outside the gates of the mansion, talking to the hundreds of fans gathered at the entrance.

"Good-evening ladies and gentlemen, we are outside the mansion in Memphis. As you can see by the hundreds of people gathered here at the gates, the world is waiting to learn the truth about the king. Is he really inside these gates or is he in Israel, fighting for his life in Maccabee Hospital? Channel Five has the latest and best news in the South and right now we are going to go into the famous home for a personal interview with him," Wayne yelled, above the screaming fans and the chanting of 'we love you'.

The next picture was live. Wayne Morris positioned himself in a smaller version of the red velvet chair and pulled his suit coat smooth at the shoulders. Hundreds of thousands of people would see this interview and he wanted to look professional.

"This is Wayne Morris talking to you live from inside the beautiful living room of the mansion. He's sitting right next to me and he's anxious to dispel the wild rumors that have been broadcast world-wide," said Wayne, as the camera panned the two men.

"Sir, please tell your fans that you are fine."

Eddie looked at the camera and gave his adoring fans one of his famous sneers and a quick laugh.

"Thank-you, Wayne. Ah jus want ta say that I'm fine and I'm happy ta be here in Memphis surrounded by all my fans. The story that I'm dyin in Israel isn't true. I've died in a few places, accordin to my critics. But, I feel great and I want to thank my fans for their concern. Ah, ah love ya."

"Ladies and gentlemen, you heard it here first on live Channel Five."

The cameras stopped rolling as the techs and Mr. Morris shook Eddie's hand and asked for autographs. Marlene stepped forward with signed pictures of him, as Eddie left the room. In the kitchen, Eddie poured himself a large glass of whiskey and shook Jerry's hand.

"Nice work."

Marlene closed the door on the news crew and hurried to the kitchen.

"Good work Eddie. Now, one more thing and you're done. Walk down to the gate and wave to your fans. Jerry will go with you and don't get too close or they will rip your arms into the metal gate. Just wave and get back up here," she ordered, straightening his jacket.

Eddie walked out the front door and down the sloping drive. He was twenty feet from the gates when the flash-bulbs began exploding in his eyes and the screams of his fans filled the air. When he was ten feet from the gate, he stopped and looked at the faces of the fans. Tears ran down the girls' faces. Teddy bears landed at his feet, as the stuffed toys were hurled over the high metal gates. Stooping to pick up a huge blue bear, he could hear the cheers from the crowd.

"Thank-you, thank-ya very much," he yelled, as he waved at this fans and turned towards the mansion.

As Eddie entered the house, he could feel the tension in the air. Marlene was seated at the kitchen table, two cigarettes were burning, one in her hand and one half-gone in the ashtray. Her face looked drawn, as she talked quietly into the telephone. Eddie stopped at the door and listened to the one-sided conversation.

"What do you mean, he's in a coma? Ya, I know it was risky. Do ya think he's goin to live? Well, what the hell did the doctor say? Ya, we got the scandal covered. Don't worry about it. You just get him out of that friggin coma and home. I know . . . I know," she said, as she hung up the phone.

"Marlene, was that a call from the hospital?

"Ya, Eddie. But, I can't talk now. Where's Someti and where the hell is Jerry?" she asked, wiping her eyes.

"I don't know where the doctor is. But, Jerry's outside. Do ya want me to get him for ya, baby?"

"No Eddie, just get out of those clothes and go back to your room. You got an early photo shoot and I don't want you to look tired."

Eddie looked at Marlene and wondered if the surgery was successful and was he going to make it. Then he wondered about himself, if he didn't make it.

CHAPTER TEN

For three days the nurses of the intensive care unit monitored a comatose patient, a patient they believed to be a legend. Guards at the door protected the entrance of anyone who was not staff. Gerda Krypka knew she was taking an awful chance, but before this idol of hers was discharged she was going to visit him. As she approached the door to the I.C.U., she stopped. Two guards stood outside the unit and a special duty nurse sat by his bed. This was not going to work. Turning on her heel, she went to the desk and asked the nurse at the desk, who the private duty nurse was in Mr. Sanders' room. The nurse looked at her uniform and said the duty nurse's name.

"Hilda Gross, I thought that was her. I think I know how I can get into that room," Gerda thought, as she glanced one more time at Hilda, her old college roommate.

Dr. Kohn, concerned over his patient's condition, ordered a brain scan. Three days was enough to regain consciousness. The fact that his patient showed no signs of recovery worried the doctor.

The scan was favorable. Normal brain activity had been detected. Even though this didn't rule out the possibility of brain damage or indicate the duration of the existing coma, the doctor brightened at the results of the test. Mr. Sanders' friends were anxious for the news of his progress and he quickly shared the results with the two men.

"Marlene, the doc says it looks like he is gettin better. He's still out cold. But, the doc says his brain is tickin. Ginny is comin in tonight. I got her some strange Indian thing to wear for a disguise. I'll let ya know when I know somethin. Oh, good luck on the concert in Vegas. Ya know I wish I was there . . . too much sand and hospitals. Can't wait to get back to Mary's cookin. Everythins Kosher or somethin here. Tell Jerry, hey!" said Chris, as he hung up the phone in the lobby of the hospital.

Eddie finished the photo shoot and packed for his trip. The jet was ready to leave at three and the concert was scheduled for tomorrow night and the next two nights. Nerves were getting the better of him. Dr. Someti was back from his trip or where ever he had went and had given Eddie a new prescription of tranquilizers. They seemed to make his head hurt and his heart felt funny. But, they did put him to sleep.

On the plane, he climbed into the bed and slept. As the plane landed, he found himself doubled over in the bathroom, vomiting.

"Maybe I'm just air sick," thought Eddie, as he forced himself out of the bathroom and off the plane to the waiting limo.

The heat of Vegas felt like a blast-furnace. Marlene and Tony didn't seem to notice. They had their eyes on the glittering Casinos that jammed the strip.

"Can't wait to hit the crap tables," said Tony, as they passed the looming Casinos.

"Just remember Tony, business first and then you can play," she teased.

"Eddie, remember you can't leave the room. If you do, the fans will tear you apart. We have arranged for the whole top floor of the Hilton and you will follow the same procedure we did in Tahoe; service elevator, kitchen and dinner theater. Tony and Jerry will be with you at rehearsal and security will handle the concert. Got it?"

Eddie nodded. His stomach was doing flips. The thought of a twelve hour rehearsal with the band and back-up singers made his mouth fill with hot water.

The Hilton in Vegas was much larger than its sister Casino in Tahoe. The suites looked the same, but the dinner theater was much larger. As Eddie walked across the stage, preparing for his rehearsal, he thought of his boss.

"Man, this is for you. I'm doin this for you."

Eddie pictured the dying old man as he swaggered off the large stage. The band was set up and the girls took their places on the stools at the far side of the stage. Eddie listened from his dressing room as the theme from 2001 played through the huge speakers. He looked at his costumes arranged in the dressing room. The blue jumpsuit with the fringe was his favorite. He'd wear it on opening night. The black pants and gold shirt he had on tonight paled against his rhinestone studded costumes. Listening to the harmony of his singer's he knew he should get out on the stage and begin this rehearsal. His stomach had settled down and the stares he had received from the hotel employees and the stage crew seemed natural to him by now.

"Then, why am I so paranoid about going out on the stage for rehearsal," he said, as he pulled a lock of his black hair down on his forehead.

"Hey man, you ready," yelled Jerry, as he tried the locked door of his dressing room.

Eddie opened the door and walked up the steps to the stage. Members of the band looked up at him. Muffled conversation traveled through the back-up singers. Eddie looked at the group of musicians, many of them known to be his bosses' close friends and left the stage.

"Shit, I can't do this. I just can't do this," he thought, as he paced around his locked dressing room.

Jerry pounded on his door, "Hey, are ya all right?"

Eddie cracked the door.

"Yah ain't fixin to fall out, are ya man?"

"Ah, no ahm all right. Just a little tard. Let's get the band to do "Fever." I think I got one," Eddie drawled, as he climbed back on the stage.

The music started, "Never know how much I love you," he sang. The melodic voices of his female back-up singers chimed in and Eddie missed his part.

"Whoa man. Hold it," Eddie laughed, as he threw up his arms.

Members of the band stared at a visibly shaken Eddie.

"I, I'll be all right. I'mah gonna go lay down, I'm all screwed up, ah ha, ya-a, all screwed up," he laughed, as he left the stage for the second time.

Back in the dressing room sweat poured down his face, chest and back.

"Shit, I just blew that," he said, as he wiped his red face on a towel.

Like a bad nightmare, Tony opened his dressing room door.

"Hey man, what's goin on? You left a lot of people wondering what's wrong with you. We got a deal, ya know?"

Eddie walked directly towards Tony, slamming him hard against the wall. With his right hand he picked the thug up from the floor and tossed the unconscious Tony out into the hall. Stage crew and bad members stood staring at a knocked out Tony. Eddie, huffing and puffing, looked at the crumbled form of Tony.

"Man, I told ya, I got a headache!" he said, as he slammed the door shut to his dressing room.

Shaking all over, he reopened the door, grabbed Tony's gun from its holster and dropped it in the toilet tank in his bathroom

"Great, great, now I'm dead. I'm dead. That's it, I'm dead. What would you do? You would finish the friggin rehearsal, wouldn't you?" he said to the empty room.

Fifteen minutes later, Eddie appeared on stage in the blue jumpsuit.

"My head feels better, let's do it," yelled Eddie.

In minutes the familiar sounds of "Fever" filled the room and this time Eddie made no mistakes. He swaggered, he sneered, he sang his heart out and when he finished the set, he left the stage and returned to his dressing room. Expecting to be gunned down by a now conscious Tony, he cautiously closed the door and slipped out of his costume.

"No use to ruin a great jumpsuit," Eddie thought, as he pictured bloody scenes from the movie "The Godfather" in his mind.

His nerves relaxed, as he changed his clothes and took another pill. With conviction, he opened the door and walked out into the auditorium. The same friendly crew, now, gave him distance, avoiding direct eye contact. His band and singers glanced briefly in his direction, as he left by the service entrance. Even Jerry didn't say anything. Tony, on the other hand, was nowhere around.

"Shit, I'm ready. I'm the boss and when I think rehearsal is over, it's over. God, I'm starvin," thought Eddie, as he swaggered from the elevator, past the smiling guards and into his penthouse suite.

News of Eddie's behavior reached Marlene. Tony wanted to break his arm and Doctor Someti insisted it was probably an adverse reaction to the new medication.

"I want both of you to stay the hell away from him. Do you understand," she said, pointing her cigarette at Tony and Someti.

"Shit, he's nobody. He thinks he's great, but if he hits me again, I'll kill the son-of-bitch," said Tony.

"You better think about it, Tony. You hurt Eddie and you can kiss a million bucks good-bye. He's our ticket to "easy street". So stay away from him or I'm shipping you back home tonight."

"Marlene, I think I can take care of his mood swings. Let me give him some new pills and they will level him out," said Someti.

"Doc, you better quit experimenting on him. Get it right this time. He's got a full house for his opening night and I don't want him walkin off stage, like he did during rehearsal."

Eddie felt much better devouring three peanut-butter and banana sandwiches and two beers. Jerry wondered if Eddie really liked the combination or if he ate the sandwiches because they were rumored to be his bosses' favorite.

Dr. Someti was sure he could handle Eddie. Pills were his specialty.

"Who needs guns, when modern medicine has so many creative forms of control," thought the doctor, as he entered Eddie's suite.

Eddie stood up from the couch, as the door opened.

"Oh, it's you," he said, still wondering if he would have to finish the thing he started with Tony.

"Well Eddie, I hear you had a headache at rehearsal. I have some vitamins I want you to start taking. They will help you avoid the stress of performing. They should give you some extra energy. Here, take a couple of them, right now, and two more before your performance."

Eddie looked at the big red capsules and wondered why they didn't look like any vitamins he had ever taken. Someti handed him a glass of water and Eddie swallowed them.

An hour later, Eddie was dancing around the suite, singing all his favorite songs as loud as he could. He was so charged-up that he couldn't sit still. By the time the make-up people arrived, Eddie was wild-eyed. He downed two more pills and tried to sit still while they worked on his hair and make-up. Twice he asked Jerry to turn up the air conditioner up higher. It was only sixty degrees in the suite, but perspiration ran down Eddie's body. He had never felt so good.

"Man, I'm ready. I'm great and I'm ready," he said, as he slipped into his blue jumpsuit.

"You look great, baby," said Marlene, as she stuck her head into Eddie's bedroom

"Look out Vegas, I'm in the house," Eddie said, as he did a quick Karate move.

The audience loved his performance. Eddie had immense energy and as his voice rocked the Hilton, the band felt his enthusiasm.

This concert was, as the critic's wrote, "A fabulous performance. The fans screamed and his love songs brought tears to the girls' eyes, as they applauded standing up on their chairs." One lucky photographer caught his exit on the last night of the three concert tour. The picture of Eddie running, as to score a touchdown, showed him jumping into the white limo. The reporter noted that he was in great health. Eddie smiled, as he read the revues.

"I'm doin this for you. Hell, I'm doin this for me. I'm as good as he is or I wouldn't be able to pull this off. I'm damn good!" he thought, as he opened the white envelope full of hundred dollar bills.

CHAPTER ELEVEN

As soon as Marlene returned home, she was immersed in the troubles in Haifa. Even though the fans in America were convinced that he was well and performing in Vegas, the fans in Israel were not. Groups of teenagers sat vigil outside Maccabee Hospital and the boys had been forced to put more guards around the I.C.U. Newspapers ran daily stories on the mysterious Mr. Sanders and General Motors Corporation had refused to comment as to the existence of an executive named Sanders. On a more serious note, the patient remained deep in a coma.

Gerda Krypka waited patiently in the lunch room for her friend Hilda Gross. It was Gerda's day off but, she had plans to work today. As Hilda approached her table, she knew she was taking a big risk. Changing I.D. badges and duty assignments was grounds for dismissal. Gerda held the twenty dollar bill in her moist hands. She couldn't be this close and miss seeing him.

"Gerda, I don't think this will work. The nurses are the weekend substitutes and they won't know you but, what if the doctor comes in. Mr. Sanders is still in a coma. So what's to see?"

"Hilda, it's just for three hours and then I will meet you back here, with your badge. Come on, a deal is a deal," she said, as she slipped her the twenty.

"O.K., but just for three hours and be careful."

Gerda took the elevator to the tenth floor, presenting her I.C.U. badge to the guards, front desk supervisor and the private duty nurse who sat next to the bed. No one questioned her, as she situated herself next to her patient. He appeared completely unconscious. The ventilator hummed quietly, as the tubes running from his bloated body kept him alive. Taking out a picture of her idol, she tried to compare his facial features. His nose seemed to match, but his skin was so stretched from the excessive water retention, that his facial features were distorted. Arranging his sheets and straightening his gown, she quickly looked at his penis. He was not circumcised. That matched. His long fingers looked right. As she pulled his gown up higher on his neck, she noticed the crescent scar on his bicep.

"Did he have a scar? She thought, as she tried to remember every fact she had read about him.

"I think I read somewhere that he did. Something about a soccer game or something."

Holding his graceful hand in hers she could feel his energy. Silently, she prayed that he would open his beautiful blues eyes and talk to her. Picking up his chart, she scanned the notes for signs of progress. Mr. Sanders had received his new liver a week ago. The surgery was a success and the body showed no signs of infection or organ rejection. However, the patient had not regained consciousness. Results of the brain scan indicated that his brain was exhibiting normal activity.

The part that interested her was his address, Memphis, Tennessee. As she replaced his chart into the slot at the end of the bed, Gerda hummed the tune "Loving You".

Combing his white hair, she talked softly to him.

"Honey, I know that you are in there. I love you. Please open your eyes and let me see those beautiful blue peepers," she said.

As she washed his arms and massaged his hands with lotion, his finger moved. Afraid to react, she continued to massage his arm. Again, this time much more stronger, his finger lifted slightly from the sheet.

"Honey, come back to us. We love you," she whispered.

A soft moan escaped his dry lips. A small flutter and his eye-lids opened a little.

"Come on baby, you can do it," she coaxed.

Another moan, this time more pronounced and then his eyes opened fully. Pursing his lips together, he tried to speak.

"Darling, you have a tube in your throat. Don't talk till I get the doctor to remove it."

Rushing from the room, Gerda alerted the staff that her patient had regained consciousness and was trying to talk.

Word spread quickly through the hospital. Fans took up the news and pushed closer against the security guards. Orthodox Jews, assured that their prayers had been answered, prayed loudly and fervently. Then the strangest of the rumors hit the *Haifa Gossip Gazette*. Afraid to print any more news about him, the article they printed stated that he had a twin brother Jesse who was alive in Israel, healed by a beam of light from a U.F.O. According to the *Gossip Gazette*, the U.F.O. had been spotted hovering above Maccabee Hospital for several minutes. These minutes, of course, were the exact time that the comatose patient had regained consciousness.

Inside the I.C.U., Dr. Kohn examined his patient. Members of the surgical team crowded the small room, as Nurse Krypka slipped the picture of her idol in her pocket and moved to an inconspicuous corner of the room shaking. He lifted his thumb to the ventilator hose and moaned.

"I believe our patient wants to breathe on his own," said the doctor happily, as he removed the tube.

Gerda held her breath as he continued breathing on his own.

"Pain," he whispered.

"Mr. Sanders, we will have you out of pain very soon. In fact, we may even have you walking again," said the doctor, writing down new orders for his patient and leaving the I.C.U.

Gerda, alone at last with her famous patient, hung the new I.V. and looked down at him. In the excitement, no one had noticed her.

Now, with less than an hour before her shift would end, she wanted to confirm that this was really him.

"Sir, I've been a big fan of yours for years."

He slowly opened his eyes and smiled.

"How long have I been here?" he whispered.

"About a week, but the doctor says you are doin great. He says you will be able to sing again. I sure pray you can. Your music has added so much to my life."

"What's your name?"

"Gerda, and everyone says you are Mr. Sanders but, I know you are using a secret cover."

"Can I have something to drink, Gerda?"

Gerda placed an ice chip on his parched lips, then she leaned forward and kissed his cheek.

"Are you him?" she whispered.

He nodded his head and closed his eyes.

"I knew it!"

As she smiled from ear to ear, the doctor re-entered the room. This time Gerda wasn't as lucky.

"Gerda Krypka, I thought that was you. Why are you working in I.C.U.? You don't do private duty work. I think I smell a deception here. I think you should work for a couple of weeks in E.R., possibly on the night shift. That way, you won't have the energy to get yourself into anymore trouble."

Gerda listened to the doctor, nodding her agreement to the punishment. After all, she had just kissed the king and would have happily worked as the janitor for that honor. Picking up her purse, she watched the new private duty nurse help Dr. Kohn with her idol's care. He was in good hands but, she had been there when he woke up and hers was the first face he had seen when he regained consciousness.

By evening, Marlene had received word that E. had regained consciousness. Ginny was on her way to the hospital and Eddie had went on a midnight buying spree with the boys at a mall in Whitehaven. Even Audrey was over her bitchy mood.

    As his health improved, physical therapy was incorporated into his program. Slowly, he sat on the side of the bed, dangling his legs over the floor. By the end of the week, the whole floor gathered to watch, as Mr. Sanders took his first steps. Although strangely silent, he eventually maneuvered the halls well. Accompanied by his ever-present guards, a lady draped in multi-colored saris, and an orderly, pulling an I.V. stand behind them, he never went unnoticed. Security was tight but somehow a large, fuzzy teddy bear made its way to his bed, as he returned from his walk. He found the bear comforting, refusing to release it even for his baths. Ginny, her saris masking her identity, sat next to his bed, only leaving his side during the doctor's frequent visits.

"Mr. Sanders, I am going to have a Dr. Millstone examine you. He is our staff psychiatrist. I would like you to talk to him about your depression," said Dr. Kohn.

The patient nodded his head. Since regaining consciousness, Mr. Sanders' physical condition had improved. But, mentally he was not alert, communicable or responsive. Even the arrival of his girl had not triggered any more response than small smile. He seemed content to lie in his bed hugging his teddy bear and watching superhero cartoons.

After the session with the doctor, Ginny expressed her fears.

"Dr. Millstone, he doesn't even seem to know me. I talk to him about things we have done together and he just lies there, playing with that stupid bear. Is he ever going to be the way he was before?"

"How long have you been with Mr. Sanders?"

"We have lived together for over a year and I have known him for almost two years. This man is a giant. He is my life and the life-force for many people. I don't know what will happen if word gets out that he is retarded."

"Young lady, those are some pretty harsh words. He has suffered some mental incapacitation from his extensive surgery and comatose state but, I would not go as far as to call him retarded. It is very possible that he will regain some, if not all of his mental abilities, over the next year. I am suggesting an extensive psychiatric program to determine the extent of his loss and to rebuild his powers of thought and speech. You, being an important part of his life, will be vital to the execution of these exercises. So, please be patient with Mr. Sanders and I am sure he will exhibit fine results."

Ginny looked at the doctor and then at her lover. She loved him and she wanted things back the way they used to be. But, maybe a year, how could it take a year? What would happen to her in a year? What would happen to his career in a year?

His hair combed, and shaved and showered, dressed in a blue sport shirt and white slacks, he looked like a patient who was recovering. Walking with the orderly's assistance, he even smiled as Ginny took his hand. This was his first time outside the hospital and he, though silent, seemed to be enjoying the bright sunlight. His silver sunglasses and ten pound weight loss revealed his true identity. Nurses gathered at the atrium windows, whispering among themselves, as he passed by them. Resting on a wooden bench, Ginny placed her tiny hands on each side of his face, as she knelt at his feet.

"I love you. You know I love you. Why don't' you talk to me?"

"Gingerbread," he said, smiling. Tears clouded her eyes. He hadn't called her Gingerbread since the surgery, a name he called her during intimate moments. At last, he was returning to the land of the living.

Exhausted, he retuned to his room. The orderly undressed him and returned him to his bed. Grabbing his teddy bear, he turned over on his side and fell into a deep sleep.

Three weeks past and his condition remained the same. During a meeting with Dr. Millstone, Ginny voiced her fears.

"Well, I did the therapy with him. Now what? He won't talk to me and doctor his eyes seem dead. I mean it's like there's nothin goin on upstairs."

"Ginny, I can only tell you that he is suffering from post-operative depression. I believe that he is ready to go home. I am suggesting that when you leave, you forget to take the bear. Its therapeutic properties are questionable. I am afraid it may be inflating his childlike fantasies. Maybe returning to his home will spur his verbal communication. I am suggesting to Dr. Kohn that Mr. Sanders be discharged in the morning."

Dr. Kohn delivered the news to his patient that evening. Looking to Ginny for instructions, he shook the doctor's hand and smiled. In the morning, Ginny packed his few possessions, hiding the bear beneath the bed, as the orderly dressed him for his discharge. Tears and handshakes greeted him as the staff stopped whatever they were doing to say good-by to Mr. Sanders. Even Chris and Don thought he looked great, as they helped him into the white limo.

"Baby, how do you feel" asked Ginny as she laid her head on his shoulder.

"I'm O.K.. I want to go home."

"Me too," she replied, as a tear slipped from her eye.

On the flight home, Ginny climbed in the private jet's bed with her man. Holding him tight, she ran her fingers over his stomach and kissed his neck. He pulled away from her and turned over on his side.

"God, I wish he would show me some affection," she thought, as she listened to his even breathing, the sign that he was fast asleep. Getting up from the bed, she walked into the main body of the plane and sat down with Don and Chris.

"He's asleep," she said.

"Ya know Gin, he looks good. I mean, he's not as loud, but he looks good," said Chris.

"I can't wait to get some hair dye on the white hair. That's the first thing I want to do," she replied.

As the plane landed in Memphis, he emerged from the bedroom. His shirt was hanging out and he looked confused. Ginny rushed to his side. Slowly, she let him back into the bedroom. With little help from him, she redressed him and combed his hair. The limo driver sat patiently at the end of the stairs. As E. and Ginny deboarded the plane, he jumped from the limo to open the door.

"Sir, it's great to have you back in Memphis. You look rested. How was your flight?"

He looked at his limo driver, expressing no recognition, and silently climbed into the car. His silver sunglasses masked his eyes. Ginny commented twice about the hot weather and the traffic, as they travelled the expressway to the Boulevard. He appeared to not hear her. The limo driver played some of his favorite spiritual music. E. sang quietly.

"At least his voice sounds the same," she thought.

A few faithful fans stood at the gates of the mansion. As the limo turned into the property, he sat further up in his seat and looked through the tinted windows at the girls. A small smile crossed his lips. Ginny looked out the window at the house as the limo swept up the long driveway.

"Home, at last," she said, as she squeezed his hand, watching as he removed the sunglasses and looked at the beautiful house.

"Baby, everythin is goin to be fine," he answered.

CHAPTER TWELVE

Hours before the king returned to the mansion, Eddie stood in the kitchen talking to Paulene, the new cook.

"Mr. Eddie, you kinda look like 'em, but you shore ain't him," she laughed, as she wiped her greasy hands on her apron and continued frying up eggs, sausage and her bosses' favorite, crispy bacon.

As Eddie filled his plate with the Southern delicacies, Marlene stormed in the back door, engulfed in her ever-present cloud of smoke from her cigarette.

"Eddie, stop eating. I have to talk to you," she said, as she took his plate and sat it on the table.

Grabbing his cup of coffee and looking longingly at his breakfast, he followed Marlene out into the back yard. A station wagon was being loaded with all his stuff from the apartment.

"Hey, what's goin on?"

"Eddie don't ask any questions. Please just get in the car. We've rented you different quarters."

"Shit, Marlene, why didn't ya let me know? Let me run up to the apartment and make sure they got all my stuff."

"No Eddie, they got it all. Just get in the car. Go . . . damn you're slow," she said, pushing him into the car and slamming the door.

The driver shot down the driveway and made a left on the Boulevard. Eddie looked out through the rear windows of the car. A long white limo was entering the gates of the mansion.

As the driver and Eddie drove through traffic, he realized for the first time in two months that he wasn't being watched. He was away from his guards, Marlene and the doctor. This sensation of freedom felt strange to him and was short lived. At the next driveway, the driver turned to his right and entered the parking lot of "The Rosebud Motel".

"Geez, I'm free and I've got a car," Eddie thought, as the driver left the car running in the parking lot and entered the motel office.

A few minutes later, the driver returned. Eddie was stunned that he had wasted his only chance of freedom. Everything was happening too fast. He needed time to think. The pills he had taken seemed to sharpen his senses, but he couldn't react. Pulling the car up to the room number three, he unloaded Eddie's gear and deposited them on the floor in a rather drab room with two double beds and a picture of the Mississippi River on the wall. Eddie started to ask the reason for his new residence, but the phone rang.

"Eddie, this is Marlene. He's here. Don't go anywhere. You're bein watched. They'll hurt you," she warned, as the line went dead.

Eddie pulled back the curtain and looked out into the parking lot. The station wagon was gone. The strange feeling of being alone was nothing compared to the thought that the king, the man he had saved, was back from the dead. Anger clouded joy. Instead of being thanked for his hard work, he was dumped in this motel. Scanning the parking lot, he tried hard to see he enemies that were supposed to be watching him. As his anger boiled, he opened the door and stepped out into the parking lot. His hands clenched into tight fists.

"Bastards, where are you?"

No one stepped from the shadows. Confidence overcame his fear. Swaggering into the center of the lot, he did his famous moves, slashing the air with sharp Karate kicks.

"Lies, she's a lyin bitch. Goddamn it, I don't need this stress."

His heart pounding, he walked to the office and approached the grey haired lady, sitting behind the counter.

"Pardon me ma'am, can y'all call me a cab?"

The little senior citizen was drinking coffee and smoking a cigarette. Jumping at the sound of his voice she looked up at his handsome face and choked on her coffee. Her cigarette fell from her open lips and landed between her legs.

"Oh my God, it's you," she yelled, as she swept her hand between her legs, pushing the cigarette onto the floor.

"Ah, I'm not who you think I am ma'am. I jus need a cab."

"Arnie, get out here. The king is in our office and he needs a cab."

Arnie, pulling up his suspenders and neglecting to zip his fly, waddled out into the office.

"Hey man, I've got a picture of you, boy," he said, clutching a dusty velvet airbrush of his likeness, complete with sweat running down his face.

A confused, frustrated Eddie, spun on his heel and walked out of the office. Surprised, he came face to face with exploding flashbulbs and screaming fans, all wanting touch him and get autographs.

"Y'all got it wrong. Man, I'm not who y'all think I am. I'm just an impersonator. See," he said as he popped out his blue contacts and showed them his light green eyes.

Dejected, he walked back to his room. He could hear the disappointment in their voices.

"I knew that wasn't the real king, he's too old," said one of the girls.

"All right folks, the show's over. Back away from the office and move your cars out of the parking lot. Make room for my customers," yelled Arnie. Soon, the parking lot of The Rosebud Motel was quiet.

Eddie took another pill and poured himself a large glass of scotch. Lying on the lumpy bed, he closed his eyes.

"I'm nothing. I'm not Eddie and I'm sure as hell not him. What am I, besides stupid?"

* *

*

For the first time in two months, the owner of the mansion walked through the front door. Present for the occasion was an odd assortment of disciples beside him, Ginny, Marlene, the remaining members of the guys, Dr. Someti and the cook. Absent was his family. Paulene was the first to embrace him.

"Sir, it's good ta have ya home. Have'n that Eddie man here was spooky. He sure ain't you."

The guys laughed at Paulene. Her dialect was country and sincere, but her large arms and huge bosom pressing against an un-responding E., startled them.

"Man, he acts like he don't know the old lady," whispered Chris.

Marlene gave them a "shut up" look, but even Dr. Someti registered concern on his face.

E. didn't seem aware of the tension. Grabbing Ginny's hand, he walked up the stairs and into his bedroom.

"Baby, I'm tired," he said, as he walked into the large bathroom and dropped his clothes onto the floor.

Obediently, Ginny picked up his monogrammed pajamas and helped him dress. Serving his every need was her job. But, in return she received what she thought was his love. Now, as she tried not to look at the ugly scar on his back, she wondered if he even wanted her there. Turning back the covers on his bed, she watched him maneuver his sore body into the bed, pulling the covers up to his neck. Dropping her clothes to the floor, she slipped in next to him. At ten-thirty an unpleasant feeling woke her. The bed was damp. Jumping from the bed, she stood staring at her sleeping man, disbelief clouding her face. Angrily, she shook him. "Honey, get up. The bed's wet and you need to get a shower."

Showing no signs of embarrassment, he obediently followed her to the shower. Quickly, she stripped his wet pajamas from his lethargic body and turned on the warm shower. As soon as the water struck his body, he left the shower and urinated in the toilet. Staring at him, she helped him back into the shower and soaped his body. Soaked and frustrated, she left him sitting on the stool by the shower, a large towel draped around his ample body.

In just a robe, she ran down to the lower level of the house. Someti was sitting in the living-room. Removing his glasses, he smiled at this nearly naked female.

"Well, by the looks of you, I would say that he's feeling frisky."

"Listen, I got a problem. He's like a zombie and he wet the bed. Doc, I need ya to help me. Come on up to his room. You'll see."

Reluctantly, Dr. Someti followed Ginny up the stairs to the bedroom. On the stool in the bathroom sat a very quiet man. His towel had slipped to the floor and his naked body didn't concern him. Ginny stared. He was very shy and his open nakedness was so strange. She remembered one time at the pool, someone had grabbed his towel from his waist. He had dove into the deep end and refused to come out of the pool, until she provided him with his swimming trunks. That was the man she knew. Not this man!

"Doc, see what I mean. He's like a damn vegetable."

"Ginny, shut up. He's not deaf. Let's get him dressed and take him downstairs to the music room."

"Hey kid, let's go downstairs and sit at the piano," said Dr. Someti, smiling.

He slipped his arms into a fresh set of pajamas and his robe. Slowly, he held onto Ginny, as the descended the stairs and entered the music room. A smile crossed his face as his hands touched the ivory keys. Tenderly he caressed them. A tune developed and he sang the first part of "The Lord's Prayer."

"Man, I can't remember the words," he said as he stood up from the piano bench and fell onto his knees on the white, furry carpet.

Marlene, Ginny, Don and Chris ran across the room towards his collapsed body. Ginny reached him first, holding his tearful face in her hands.

"I'm sorry Gingerbread. I don't feel so good. Can I lay down?"

Tears streaming down her face, Ginny ran out the front door, as Dr. Someti, Chris and Don helped him up the stairs and back into his bed. Marlene followed Ginny out the door.

"Get a hold of yourself. No one must know his condition. He'll be O.K. Just get in the house and keep your mouth shut," Marlene yelled, as she shook Ginny gently by the shoulders.

"I, I'm sorry. I just love him so much and he doesn't even seem to know me," she said, as she followed Marlene into the house and poured herself a drink.

Marlene just shook her head in disgust and climbed the stairs.

Opening the door, she watched the doctor as he administered a shot to the king.

"How's he doin?"

"This should knock him out. Did ya get the bitch calmed down?"

"Ya, she's in the kitchen, drinking straight vodka."

Marlene watched as E. began to shake violently.

"Shit, what's he doin?"

"Goddam, it's a seizure. Get something to put in his mouth."

Unfortunately, it was too late. Thrashing, biting his tongue, blood pouring from his gaping mouth, his huge frame lifted from the wet bed, bending into a distorted arc.

"Mamma, satin, mamma," he moaned as the blood and vomit gushed from his mouth, flying across the blankets and onto the floor.

"Do something," screamed Marlene.

Dr. Someti looked at her face and picked up a large pillow from the blood splattered carpet. Veins bulged in his thin neck as he pressed the pillow over the king's face. A scream stuck in Marlene's throat. Someti, his face contorted, pressed harder, lifting his thin frame off the floor. Seconds passed, then as the large frame of E. fell limp on the bed, Dr. Someti, his eyes still bulging, stood up. In his hands he looked at the murder weapon and slowly released it from his clenched fists.

Marlene fell on her knees next to the bed. Her hands clawed at the soiled carpeting.

Ginny, her drink still in her hand, climbed the stairs to their bedroom. As her eyes adjusted to the dim light of the room, she screamed. Her lover, soaked in vomit and blood, with his mouth contorted, his eyes frozen, a severed piece of tongue on his cheek, lay in a contorted pose on his bed. Beside him stood Someti. As he lifted his blood-spattered face and smiled a maniacal smile, Ginny released her hold on her glass and heard it shatter to the floor. Suddenly, she felt Marlene's claw-like fingers grab her ankle. Kicking and screaming, she saw Marlene collapse at her feet. Turning, she ran from the room and down the steps into the living room. An animalistic scream pierced the air, as she clawed at the phone. Suddenly, she was lifted off the floor, as a sharp blow across her face slammed her into the wall. Limp and unconscious, Dr. Someti rolled Ginny's tiny frame on her stomach. Someti, now on his knees, gasped for breath, as he ripped his tie from his neck and bound her hands tightly behind her back. Grabbing her around the waist he dragged her to the hall closet and stuffed her in the dark compartment. Exhausted, he sat spread-legged on the floor of the foyer.

Marlene descended the stairs, dragging her soaked blouse behind her, wearing only her slacks and shoes.

"Call an ambulance. Get help. You killed him, you bastard. You killed him. Oh my God, you killed him," she screamed, as she launched herself from the last step onto his body, pounding her fists into his face.

As they rolled over and over on the tile entrance, Someti grabbed Marlene's throat and squeezed. Clawing at his eyes, she felt her hands slide from his face. A sharp light flashed in her mind, as he slammed her head hard against the floor. The house was deathly still. Dr. Someti stepped over Marlene and walked into the bathroom. His face was covered with blood and long scratches extended down his pale cheek. His shirt was torn and covered with vomit and blood. He resembled a man who had survived a car crash.

"Think, think. You can get out of this," he said, as he splashed his face with cold water.

Staggering through the carnage of E.'s bedroom, he picked up the phone receiver and called Jerry.

"Hi Jerry, this is Someti. Oh, I think he will be fine. It will just take a while. Listen, I need you to run over to The Rosebud Motel. Eddie's in room three. Don't let him leave. Spend the night. We might have a small problem."

"Aw Doc, do I have to . . . O.K. But, I did have plans," said Jerry.

"Jerry, just do it. The next meds are on me."

"Ya, O.K. Doc, have you been joggin? You sure are puffin. Hello? Hello? Shit, he must of hung up."

Someti picked up his gun from the floor by the bed and walked down the steps to the front door. The place was deserted. Breathing deeply, he let his conniving mind run free.

Lifting her sore head from the cold tiles, Marlene gently looked around. Seeing no one, she stood up and opened the front door. From the shadows of the large carved column, Someti emerged. Marlene found herself looking down the barrel of his gun. Carefully, she backed through the door and into the entrance hall. Someti, never lowering his weapon, followed her into the house. A strange glint in his insane eyes made her shiver.

"Listen to me. This is great. This will work," he muttered, as he walked around her in a circle, running his hand through his thin hair.

"What? You're crazy. You're a murderer," she hissed, as she turned around, afraid to take her eyes off the gun.

Abruptly halting in front of her, she watched as an evil smile crossed his lips. "Listen to me you dumb bitch! We can be rich beyond our wildest dreams."

"Shut up," Marlene screamed, as she placed her hands over her ears. Tears streamed down her face as she looked at her blood-stained hands. "I have blood in my hair. I'm callin the police!"

"Marlene, I'll kill you . . . I'll kill Audrey. A lesbian quarrel. What a shame. Of course, those kinds of relationships are a blasphemy. If you ask me, they are better off dead," cackled Someti, as he lit a cigarette with one hand, still holding the gun on Marlene with the other hand.

Marlene looked at his eyes. "He means it . . . God, what have I done?" she thought.

CHAPTER THIRTEEN

Marlene stood very still for several seconds.

"Give me a cigarette," she said, as she looked at Someti. "And put away that friggin gun."

"We could all go to jail," she said calmly, as she walked into the living room and sat down on the couch.

Someti followed her into the room and stood in front of her, his hands on his hips.

"Not if you listen to me, Marlene. First call the cook and give her a week off."

"But, she will wonder why?"

"Just do it. Make up something. Start using all the bullshit you give out!"

"All right, I'll get rid of her and the groundskeeper."

Someti walked to the closet. He could hear Ginny moving around. "I'm not goin to be beat up again. Go upstairs to the bedroom and get my medical bag," ordered Someti.

"What? Upstairs to his room? I can't," moaned Marlene, thinking of the contorted body on the bed and the smell of vomit in the room.

"Shit Marlene, get up there or I'll shoot you now," yelled Someti, reaching into his pocket for his gun.

Marlene tried not to look at the horror-stricken eyes of her boss, as she quickly moved around the bed to the bathroom. The sweet, sickening smell of blood and urine filled the room. She could feel the warm water rising in her throat as she opened the bathroom door. Vomiting into the toilet, she thought about calling the police. As she looked in the mirror, she changed her mind. Her hair was caked in dried blood and her chest had large purple bruises running all the way up to her neck. Grabbing a robe from the back of the door, she slipped it on and pulled it high over the purple and black marks. Wetting a towel, she tried to wipe some of the blood from her hair and face. Tears streamed down her cheeks as she grabbed the black bag from the floor of the bathroom and retuned to the living room. Ginny was kicking frantically at the closet door and crying hysterically.

"Grab her feet when I open the door. Sit on her if you have to. I am going to give her something and then we won't have to deal with her," ordered the doctor, as he opened the door and stood back.

Marlene looked at Ginny's scared face and whispered, "Just relax, don't kick and you won't die." Ginny closed her eyes and curled up into a fetal position. Someti injected her with the syringe and closed the door.

"Good, now make those calls and meet me upstairs. Remember, no tricks or Audrey will be as dead as you."

"Geez, what a stench," said the doctor as he opened a few windows and turned on a fan.

"Marlene" said the doctor over the intercom. Marlene jumped, dropping the phone to the floor.

"God, you scared the shit out of me," she yelled into the unit on the wall. "What?"

"Go out to the carport and see if you can find something to wrap the body in. Maybe a tarp, or a car cover. Hurry up! I'm getting hungry," yelled the doctor.

The thought of food gagged her and she threw up outside the back door. Pawing through the car supplies, she saw a large painter's tarp rolled up against the tire of the golf cart. It hadn't been driven since the divorce.

Marlene's thoughts were interrupted by Someti.

"That's the ticket. Grab the other end and we will haul it upstairs and roll the body off the bed onto it."

"Isn't it a beautiful day? Too bad, I'm so busy," thought Someti, as the sun shown down on the two of them.

Marlene laid the tarp down on the floor next to the bed. Then she went around to the other side of the bed. Placing her hands on the scarred back, she pushed.

"Damn it, get over here and help me," she yelled.

"Let me straighten out his arms or we are never going to get him to roll on the floor."

A sickening, cracking sound filled the quiet room. Dr. Someti deftly pulled the corpse's arm flat, away from his contorted face. Then with all their strength, they pushed the body off the bed and onto the black tarp. Once the vinyl had been positioned around the body, Someti tied the bundle securely with rope.

"There, just as neat as a Christmas package," he chirped, as he smiled down at the bound and wrapped body.

"Now help me get him to the stairs. He must weigh three hundred pounds."

Grabbing his head and shoulders, Marlene and Someti pulled the body to the landing. Marlene had placed her ever-present cigarette between her lips and as she puffed and pulled, the ashes rained down on the plastic tarp.

"Damn it, you're goin to set us on fire with that cigarette. Don't you know those things are bad for your health," said Someti.

"Ya, and I suppose committing murder isn't?"

Exhausted, they sat down on the landing and both looked at the steep staircase.

"Let's get this over with," said Marlene, pulling the body towards the edge of the stairs.

Stepping onto the top step, Marlene pulled his feet towards her. Suddenly her slender heel on her pumps snapped. Grabbing the body to keep from falling backwards down the stairs, the vinyl-clad corpse gave way and together they were hurled towards the landing below. Marlene felt the slick plastic body-bag push hard against her, as it gained speed. Then, as her own body rolled over and over down the carpeted steps, she heard the soft, thick sound as her head came to rest on the rubber-wrapped head of her boss.

"Well, I guess there's more than one way to skin a cat. That sure was easier on my back. You O.K.?" said Someti, as he slowly walked down the stairs.

Marlene stood up and looked at Someti. Rage filled her face. The body had cushioned her fall. But, her nerves were raw.

"Get down here you asshole. We're not done yet. Let's put him by the pool until it gets dark. Tonight, we can give him a proper burial."

As Someti surveyed their handy-work he smiled. A black vinyl package, approximately six feet tall, lay next to the pool equipment. Hoses, pool cleaning equipment and old lawn chairs blended around the corpse. Satisfied that the body was safe, he returned to the house. As he fixed himself a sandwich in the kitchen he could hear the sounds of a rug scrubber working in the bedroom above him.

Marlene, sickened at the sight of bodily fluids, closed her eyes as she stripped the bed and filled the rug scrubber. Using the upholstery attachment, she cleaned the mattress. Pine cleaner freshened the room and the scrubber cleaned the carpet. The smell of bleach came from the washer and dryer as the doctor washed the linen. By dark, all the evidence was destroyed, except for the body. Several times during the day the phone had rung and Marlene hoped that the caller was only a friend of Ginny's, or an office call. After her next task of burying the body, she would take a shower, make some coffee and answer the calls.

Someti was asleep in the laundry room. Marlene thought about calling the police or climbing into her car and just driving away. "That son-of-a-bitch would hunt me down and bury me."

As she slammed the dryer door, Someti opened his eyes.

"Are you done?"

"Ya, now let's get the damn body buried. How are we goin to do it? You're the murderer. Got any ideas?" she hissed.

"Sweet cheeks, I've got it all figured out. Go get the station wagon and back it up to the pool gate. I got a piece of chain in the back. We'll wrap it around the body and drag it out the horse barn."

"The horse barn? Are you nuts? The stable man will be here next week and he will discover it."

"Relax. I can use a backhoe. I'll dig a hole in the soft ground under his favorite horse's stall and then he will always be with a friend. It's kinda sweet, don't you think?"

"I think you are a homicidal maniac. But, let's get this done. I'm smelling as bad as the body."

Marlene pulled the car up to the gate. The chains were hooked around the body and unceremoniously pulled across the manicured grounds. Gas belched from the tractor and an hour later a large hole was dug in the soft ground at the farthest end of the deep stall. Marlene, crusted in mud and wild-eyed, frantically pulled the increasingly heavy body slowly across the soft ground, letting the doctor take most of the weight. As a final thud was heard the body disappeared into the dark hole.

"Wait," Someti ordered. "We need to say a few final words. Please show some respect Marlene and bow your head."

For a second Marlene though how easy it would be to push Someti into the open grave. As if he sensed her thoughts, he stepped back a few feet from the edge and stared at her.

"Dear God, please accept our brother, and bless the new one because we deserve to be rich. Thank-you, thank-you very much," laughed Someti, returning to the backhoe and starting up the engine.

"I swear I'll kill you, Someti. I'll kill you and bury your crazy ass out here, you rotten son-of-a bitch," she screamed over the roar of the tractor.

Someti parked the tractor and retraced his steps, making sure that everything was cleaned up.

"Marlene, go get a shower and wash your hair. You look crazy in that robe," yelled Someti.

Marlene found an unused bedroom and did as she was told. Someti was nuts and she didn't want to die and be buried in the barn.

The shot Ginny had received really made his next job much easier. He took the pillow from the sofa and shot her twice in the head. Tearing the coats from their hangers, he bundled her up and carried her small dead body to the barn.

"My, my, my, you're a lucky bastard to be buried with your girlfriend," he thought, as he threw he coat wrapped corpse into the grave. Guess this grave is full. Dirt was dumped to the top and softly patted down, as Someti danced on the soft grave.

The horse was returned to the stall and all was well, as the sun set on another day.

CHAPTER FOURTEEN

Except for the Pine Sol and bleach smell, E.'s bedroom and bath were spotless. Marlene had worked her butt off. She was pleased that she had showered and washed her hair. Borrowing a blow dryer, make-up and a loose fitting pants outfit from Ginny, she began to imagine this whole day as just a bad dream. Indian clothes are so comfortable, she thought as she dialed Tammy's phone number.

"Guess what, you've earned a week's vacation. So stay home till I call you back to work. We are having the office fumigated for water bugs. Tammy was thrilled and she silently thanked the roaches for her vacation.

The next few calls resembled Tammy's and no one complained.

Marlene heard a shower running and figured Someti had decided to clean up and change. He was in Jerry's room. Hope he could find a weasel outfit in the closet to fit him. Her cigarettes were not calming her. Feeling good she entered the dark kitchen, grabbed a piece of pecan pie and a large scotch. Sitting at the kitchen table, she listened to the peacefulness of the humming of the refrigerator. Her brain was fried and slowly the scotch calmed her nerves. She laid her head on the table and began to doze off.

Before she could fall completely asleep, the bright kitchen light was turned on and Someti came walking in. He laughed, "You look like that girl on "I Dream of Jeannie." Oh well, at least you don't smell."

"Same to you asshole, at least you look better. Clothes seem to be a bit big. Oh well, it's hard to dress a prick."

The doctor never heard her. He was busy pouring himself a drink and making a sandwich. With the drink half gone, he filled it again and sat down across the table from Marlene. "Boy, I'm going to sleep like a baby tonight," Someti said. "Two killings in one night is a record for me."

Marlene popped her eyes wide open and ran to the coat closet. Ginny was gone. "You murderous bastard, why did you kill her?"

Someti smiled. "I did it as a final present for our ex-boss, sort of a going away gift. I had the hole dug and he did look lonely without Gingerbread," he laughed. "Don't worry Marlene, she could have never kept our little secret. Here's hoping you can," he said finishing his drink.

"You sleep too tonight, sweet cheeks. Tomorrow we deal with Jerry and Eddie," he said heading into Jerry's room and pulling the covers over him. He placed his gun close to his pillow and quickly went to sleep.

Eddie was happier, now that Jerry was there. They ordered pizza, beer and chips from the 7-11 next door and Jerry went and picked it up. The Steelers game was just starting when Jerry had arrived. Marlene had called, sounding panicked, said something about Jerry coming over and he should not, under any circumstances leave his room at The Rosebud.

Eddie was feeling sad. He missed the mansion, or at least the sound of the horses and his gym room at the club. "My God, these fans must have radar, to see me in that dusty old motel office, Eddie thought, "Good thing I had a little hush money for that old lady and her husband, or I would have been gone. The contact trick was my best plan, even though Marlene would have killed me with her bare hands, if she'd known what I had done. My life, my simple K-Mart life is gone. I am him." Eddie sang the words to "Why Me Lord," as he replaced his blue contacts and changed into a red velvet shirt and black pants.

A short knock on the motel door and Jerry entered with boxes of pizza, beer, chips and chocolate bars. Dropping the sacks and boxes on the small table, he went into the bathroom to wash his face. It was hot and sticky in the South. He thought about getting a shower, but the Steelers were warming up and the pizza did smell good.

As he left the bathroom, he looked in the mirror. "What kinda crazy mess am I in?" he worried.

Three hours later, they both left fine. It's amazing the recovery powers contained in twenty-four cans of beer, four pans of pizza and two candy bars, topped off with the Steelers winning. The food, for the first time in weeks, stayed in Eddie's stomach. He actually felt sleepy and safe with Jerry there.

"Goin to catch a little shut eye," he told Jerry. Jerry just nodded his head. He was reading a new "Tits and Tail" magazine and smoked a small cigar. It wasn't hard for Jerry to adapt to anything, after working for his boss and Marlene for so many years.

The only time, he could remember flat refusing to do something, was when his boss wanted him to hire a hit may to kill his cheating wife. The whole group grabbed him and Dr. Someti gave him a shot. The boss slept for nine hours and woke up much better. Meanwhile, his wife and child were moved to another coast and Jerry was sure, her boyfriend wasn't far behind. Since then everything was run by Marlene. The spark of life had left the king and he was never the same. Ginny moved in and Marlene started her search for an impersonator who looked, sounded and sang like the man.

    Dr. Someti was always present to keep him sedated and to finally take the giant step of trying to get him help. He knew he was dying and many times you could hear him talking to his momma in his bedroom. All the rest of the family had been well threatened and well paid to never set foot on the grounds again. In fact, up until yesterday everything was O.K.

    Jerry heard the phone ring in the dingy motel room. Wiping the sleep from his eyes, he answered it on the third ring. It was Marlene, she ordered Eddie and him back home immediately.

    While the boys cleared out of The Rosebud, Marlene listened to her messages. They were all from Audrey. The last one was the most interesting, "Marlene, I've met someone else and I'm moving out. Don't try to contact me." A smile crossed her lips as she opened a new carton of cigarettes, lit one, puffed deeply and contemplated the arrival of Eddie.

Jerry and Eddie arrived at the gates about ten minutes later. Marlene had changed back into her clothes, clean and fresh. She also had super glued her heel back on her shoe. Quickly, she surveyed the upstairs with a garbage bag in her hand. Ginny's make-up, clothes, and any cigarette butts were removed. Jerry's shower was checked and the living room, kitchen and barn looked fine. The horse groomer was there and spoke no English, so a smile convinced her, that everything was in perfect order.

Someti, coffee cup in one hand, and newspaper in the other greeted Jerry and Eddie as they entered the front door.

Eddie felt funny in the house, like he was going to have Marlene yell at him any minute. The coffee smelled good and he hurried into the kitchen. The cook wasn't there, but donuts and coffee was fine with him.

Someti said hi to Eddie and didn't get up from the table. Eddie grabbed doughnut, not jelly, from the box and filled a cup with coffee.

"So how goes it doc," Eddie said being friendly.

"Same old thing, nice day though," replied Someti, never lifting his eyes from the Dow Jones section of the paper.

"Where's Marlene," asked Eddie. A voice was heard from the side door. It was Marlene.

"Open this damn door, it's locked," she yelled. Someti never moved.

Eddie, afraid of the woman, jumped to his feet and ran to the side door. Unlocking the latch, he stood back as an angry Marlene stormed in. Seeing Eddie, she changed her anger to sweetness. "Honey, I thought you were gone from me, as she kissed him on the lips."

He braced himself against her body and hugged her. "Come in the kitchen. Did Jerry take good care of my stud muffin?" Marlene said, pushing Eddie off her and rushing past him to the kitchen. "Good," thought Marlene. Someti was gone and she was way too busy for him. She poured her coffee while talking a hundred miles an hour. "The private plane is ready, your clothes and crew are already at the Hilton and you leave in about twenty minutes," she barked. She hadn't even sat down at the table and his head was already pounding.

Jerry knew what to do. It was the same routine, only E. was Eddie. He was already at the plane and before Eddie's donut could digest, he was on his way to Las Vegas and a couple more hours of rest in the bedroom. Everything was planned out and routine. Eddie was excited to be back in the Hilton and he noticed that he didn't need those crazy red pills. He flew through rehearsal. His voice was rested and he didn't feel like his heart was going to beat itself to death.

The show was sold out and all his needs were met except for the beer, it was Dr. Pepper only. His make-up girls and dresser were expert and he still kept the temperature in the large suite to about 60 degrees. They all called him sir and he felt great.

Marlene was an hour behind him, in a small private jet. She had returned home to her apartment, to see it trashed and the words cheater scrawled on her wall in the bathroom. Digging through the mess, she located three suits, a swimsuit, 2 pairs of heels and casual shorts, sandals and underwear. Next, she entered the creepy bathroom. Thank goodness she bought in bulk as half of the make-up was destroyed. The new stuff she threw in a bag and was set. Last thing, she called the maid, laid out on the table double the fee, plus tip and left money to have the locks changed. On her way out she ripped the phone from the wall and stuck the receiver in the outside garbage bin. Her car broke all the speed limits, but she reached the plane on time. Crew greeted her.

"Empty the trunk and pack my clothes please?" she asked as she prepared for take-off. How she wished she had her Vitamin K shot to help her through. "Oh well," she thought, "Nobody ever gets ahead in the world by sitting, smoking cigarettes and looking through your front window. You've got to get out there and do, do, do!"

The plane landed before she had time to smoke over two cigarettes, and she chugged down the rest of her scotch, as the town car pulled up at the executive airport. People scurried by her with her fancy luggage. In the car she adjusted her scarf to cover those awful bruises. She also added a hat and large black sunglasses to her ensemble. Now, the red lipstick and a breath mint. She was fine, she looked rich, and, guess what, she was. She was met at the underground security elevator by two nice men, with guns. Already... she felt great.

Eddie's show was at ten-thirty p.m. and she hoped Someti wasn't there to dope him. Marlene didn't need two dead stars.

Arriving at Eddie's suite, she told the crew to unpack her stuff in the adjoining suite. Marlene had no desire to share a suite with Eddie.

Eddie was asleep and God did he look like E., "Eddie sweety, hate to disturb you, but it's Marlene."

Eddie opened his eyes and smiled that crooked smile she loved. "Hi baby, come on in."

Marlene continued talking, "Eddie we have some good and bad news for you."

"Tell me the good news," said Eddie.

"Well honey, our boss did not survive the surgery. We had all prayed that he would, but you saw him. What a terrible loss," she said, tears running down her cheeks. Eddie teared up too, wondering how this could be the good news. "You are the new man, permanently, if you want it. Don't think Eddie, do it for him."

"Well Marlene, I feel so empty. But my fans need me. So, it's the least I can to, right?"

She quickly agreed, checking the time on her Rolex.

"Time to get ready, you solved the bad news by saying yes. Your fans await you and as my momma used to say, 'Good endings are all that count. Your can start out poorly and end up on top of the world, or you can stay poor forever and miss your fate.' You're a talented man E. Remember, it's our little secret forever," as she kissed him on the lips.

Made in the USA
San Bernardino, CA
19 April 2015